GIRLS' N

ง

COPYRIGHT © 2016 BY JENNA ST. JAMES.
PUBLISHED BY JENNA ST. JAMES
COVER DESIGN BY JULIANA BUHMAN

JENNA ST. JAMES BOOKS

Ryli Sinclair Mystery Series (cozy)

Picture Perfect Murder   *Bachelorettes and Bodies*
Girls' Night Out Murder   *Rings, Veils, and Murder*
Old-Fashioned Murder   *Next Stop Murder*
Bed, Breakfast & Murder   *Gold, Frankincense & a Merry Murder*
Veiled in Murder   *Heartache, Hustle, & Homicide*

Sullivan Sisters Mystery Series (cozy)

Murder on the Vine   *PrePEAR to Die*
Burning Hot Murder   *Tea Leaves, Jealousy, & Murder*

Copper Cove Mystery Series (cozy)

Seaside & Homicide

A Witch in Time Series (paranormal)

Time After Time
Runaway Bride Time (novella)

A Trinity Falls Series (romantic comedy)

Blazing Trouble
Cougar Trouble

DEDICATION

To James…thanks for letting me use you as a character. And thanks for making murder so much fun. Not many couples can say they act out murder scenes to make sure everything is done right!

CHAPTER 1

"I know," Aunt Shirley said as she waved her margarita glass through the air. "How about 'I don't do windows or dinners or dishes.'" She slapped her knee in glee. "Sounds pretty darn catchy to me."

Paige threw down her pen. "Ryli, shut her up, please."

I hid my smile behind my margarita glass and shot my great-Aunt Shirley a mock glare. She retaliated by taking a long swallow of her margarita.

My best friend, Paige, was marrying my brother, Matt, in eight days on New Year's Eve. To make matters even more stressful, they weren't doing it in our hometown. They had decided to get married at my mom's lake house down in South Missouri. We'd all grown up visiting my grandparents there, and now that mom owned the house, we continued going every chance we got.

"Just say what you feel," I said. "Don't worry so much about putting it down on paper. You two have been in love since elementary school. Well, you have anyway, Matt just didn't know he was."

Paige laughed. "You're right." She took a dainty sip of her margarita. "I guess I'm just worried I'll freeze and forget what to say."

"Did I ever tell you girls Clint Eastwood once asked me to marry him?" Aunt Shirley announced.

4

I've heard these ridiculous stories a thousand times. "No, he didn't, Aunt Shirley."

"Of course, I had to turn him down. His dog's farts nearly took the paint off the walls." Aunt Shirley took another drink. "I couldn't see myself tied down to that kind of mess."

Paige giggled.

Aunt Shirley brushed her short, white hair off her face and belched. "I jusssss wanna know one thing…do we have the party covered?"

"Oh yeah," I grinned, enjoying the look of discomfort on Paige's face. "The bachelorette party is covered."

"Tell me you aren't doing anything cheesy and vulgar," Paige demanded.

Aunt Shirley hiccupped then laughed. "Those are the two ingredients needed for a good party." She downed the last of her drink and tipped dangerously in her chair.

I shook my head. "I'll never tell."

Paige groined and plunked her head down on my dining room table. Miss Molly, my black and white long-haired cat, stopped cleaning herself to glare at Paige. I was pretty sure Miss Molly knew I was leaving for a week. Every time I looked at her she either turned her back to me or started cleaning herself. That's cat language for *"You are dead to me!"*

Aunt Shirley and I were supposed to be putting the finishing touches on our list of things to take with us to the lake house on Monday, while Paige was to be working on her vows. None of us were getting very far.

Well, that's not totally true…we were pretty far down in our cups. I think this was our second pitcher of margaritas.

Aunt Shirley held up her empty glass. "I need another drink."

I obliged, but was smart enough to only fill it halfway. I figured she wouldn't notice. Seeing as how she was near Methuselah's age—a slight exaggeration—the doctor said she was supposed to drink more red wine for health reasons. Of course, Aunt Shirley's response was something along the lines of the doctor could kiss her lily-white you-know-what before she'd drink wine over tequila.

This explains why, on a frigid Saturday afternoon, two days before Christmas, we were three sheets to the wind. I'm totally blaming my aunt for this.

My great-aunt Shirley is a seventy-something retired private investigator—a virtually unheard of profession for females during her time. She worked mostly in Los Angeles from the early sixties until she retired a few years back. Which is why we constantly have to listen to her I-used-to-date-a-movie-star-way-back-when stories she enjoys fabricating.

I love her crass, no-nonsense sort of way. That *and* the fact she's given me her most prized possession—a 1965 turquoise Falcon that has a glass-like finish and dark purple ghost flames that dance across the hood and side panels—doesn't hurt, either.

Paige lifted her head off the table. "Mom and I are running to Kansas City tomorrow to get a few last-minute items. Did you want to go?"

I shook my head. "I can't. I have to finish an article for Hank, and then we're going to work on the layout for next week's paper. He's still a little grumpy that Mindy and I are taking off the whole week."

I work for the *Granville Gazette* as an investigative journalist, photographer, copy editor, and whatever else Hank needs. Hank is the owner of the *Gazette*. I always describe him the same way to everyone. He's a "Kill 'em all, let God sort 'em out" guy. A retired Marine who still walks the walk and talks the talk. Once a Marine, always a Marine. Oorah!

His wife, Mindy, is the complete opposite. Where he is mean and vulgar, she's sweet and kindhearted. She dresses like Naomi Harper from *Mama's Family*. She loves bright colors, Capri pants, and off-the-shoulder shirts and sweaters. But that's where the comparisons stop. Mindy is actually the smartest, most levelheaded woman I know outside of my own momma. Any woman who can put up with Hank has to be.

Lately Hank's been giving me more responsibilities around the office. I guess he figured since his star reporter single-handedly took down the town killer a couple months back, perhaps I could do more than write fluff pieces for his paper. Of course, I'm sure it doesn't hurt I'm currently dating the Chief of Police in Granville, either. Hank is hoping I'll scoop something for him. He can keep hoping…it'll never happen.

Garrett Kimble and I started seeing each other when we were working the last case together. Okay, that may be a stretch. He was working it, and I was getting in the way. But in the end, it brought us together. We've been "a little more than casual" for two months now.

"It's going to be awful shopping on Christmas Eve," I said.

"I know. I'm beginning to think a New Year's Eve wedding wasn't such a good idea."

"Nonthens!" I looked over at Aunt Shirley. Her near-empty margarita glass was tilting dangerously to the side, and she was rocking ever so slightly back and forth. It's official…she was smashed. "Besss idea. Gonna be specular…spectlar." Her brow furrowed. "Gonna be great!"

I rolled my eyes. "You're cut off!"

Aunt Shirley smiled wickedly at me. "Sean Connery once said those exact words to me after a night of passion. Guess I was too much a woman for him!"

I shuddered. *Great, now I'll never be able to lust after Sean Connery again!*

I turned back to Paige. "So once you get these last-minute items, you're all set?"

"I think so." Tears welled in her eyes. "I just can't believe in a few days I'm going to be Mrs. Paige Sinclair."

"Me, either," I said and wiped tears from my own eyes. "I've been dreaming of this moment just as long as you have."

"I feel like I'm at a dang funeral," Aunt Shirley mumbled.

Paige laughed. "Who's taking her home?"

Plop! Plop!

I looked down at the notification on my phone. It was a text from Garrett. "*Heard u r going over wedding plans & drinking margaritas. Be there shortly to take Paige & Aunt Shirley home safely.*"

"Looks like Garrett's coming to our rescue," I said. "He's the designated driver today."

"Oh joy," Aunt Shirley grumbled.

I glared at her. "I'm tired of having to tell you to play nice."

8

Aunt Shirley grinned. "You wanna know who played nice? Clint Eastwood. He played real nice with my—"

"Enough!" I cried.

Aunt Shirley slapped the table and cackled like a drunken hyena.

Paige and I spent the next few minutes jotting down words to incorporate into her vows. Aunt Shirley drank and vetoed all our suggestions.

The doorbell was music to my ears. I got up to answer the door, excited to see Garrett. He was about ten years older than me, had jet-black hair styled short from his military days, and piercing blue eyes. After he left active duty, he joined the Kansas City Police Department where he worked for almost eight years. It was my brother, Matt, who got Garrett his current job in Granville. They had met in Kansas City at a Veteran's function and hit it off.

"You look relatively sober," Garrett chuckled as he leaned down to kiss me.

"Wait until you see Aunt Shirley," I said. "I tried to give her some coffee to help sober her up, but she wouldn't drink it."

Garrett rolled his eyes. "No surprise there."

"I don't need no taxi." Aunt Shirley pushed herself up from the table, took two steps and stumbled. She grabbed the back of my recliner. "I'm fine."

"I don't think so," Garrett said.

Aunt Shirley narrowed her eyes at him. "The day I can't hold my liquor is the day you need to take me out back and shoot me!"

Music to my ears!

Garrett grabbed Aunt Shirley's arm and gently eased her toward the door. "From your mouth to God's ears, Aunt Shirley."

"When I was younger," Aunt Shirley told Garrett as she bundled up in her winter coat, "cops would come to *me* for suggestions on how to capture criminals."

"I'm sure they did," Garrett said patiently.

"I knew most of the cops on the LAPD. Good guys." Aunt Shirley fumbled with her coat buttons. "I miss those times."

I wrapped Aunt Shirley's scarf around her wrinkled neck. "I know you do." And I'm sure she did. I've been worried about her constant reminiscing of the past lately. She always sounds so sad.

Garrett leaned down and kissed me on the cheek. "I'll stop by after I get off work."

"Thanks. And I'll make it up to you. I promise."

Garrett gave me a wolfish grin. "You bet you will, Sin."

I shivered. I loved when he called me that.

CHAPTER 2

"Ryli Jo Sinclair, what do you think you're doing?" Paige demanded.

I shoved my overnight bag into the trunk of the Falcon then turned around. "Nothing."

"I swear, between you and Aunt Shirley, there better not be anything naughty at my bachelorette party!"

I rolled my eyes. *It's a bachelorette party, not a convent reunion for nuns.*

I looped my arm through hers and we walked back toward Mom's house. Light snow flurries were swirling in the air, but the accumulation was still less than an inch. I figured roads to the lake house would be pretty clear.

"There you two are," Matt said as we walked in the house. "We were wondering where you'd run off to."

"Just loading the last of the suitcases I brought over to Mom's yesterday. I figured she'd have more room in the Tahoe than I do in the Falcon."

Paige looked up. "Look where we are," she whispered to Matt.

Matt glanced up and grinned. He pulled Paige to him and kissed her long and hard.

I sighed loudly. Nothing.

I tapped my toes. Nothing.

I coughed. Nothing.

I turned to go find Garrett and Mom. Garrett had taken Aunt Shirley home after we finished Christmas dinner so she could finish packing. I was picking her up to leave as soon as I left Mom's. I'm not sure how I got stuck driving with Aunt Shirley the four hours to the lake house—okay, not exactly true. It was her car, so she should probably ride in it. But still…it's like I drew the short straw.

Garrett walked into the living room carrying a piece of pumpkin pie smothered in whipped cream. I sidled up to him, hoping for a bite.

Garrett moved the plate out of my reach. "No way."

I growled at him. He leaned in and kissed me quickly on the lips.

He tasted good…like pumpkin pie and coffee.

I laid my head on his chest. "Thank you for watching Miss Molly while I'm away this week." I was still nervous about leaving her, even though she'd be with Garrett. Miss Molly had recently undergone an extensive hospital stay when she was poisoned. She still gets skittish and cries if I leave her alone.

But since Garrett wasn't going to be able to drive down to the lake house until the day of the wedding, we both agreed this was the best solution. His job as the Chief of Police kept him pretty busy—especially around the holidays.

"Are the cars packed and ready to go?" Mom asked as she breezed into the room rolling a suitcase in each hand.

"The Falcon is," I said. "I'm picking up Aunt Shirley and Mindy in an hour and then driving straight there."

"Mom and I are leaving around five," Paige confirmed.

"Oh, look who came up for air," I said sarcastically.

Matt gave me a smug look. "You're just jealous."

My brother, an EMT and firefighter, had recently surprised us all by announcing that as soon as he and Paige were married, he'd be quitting his job to go to the police academy. After the brutal murders a few months ago, Officer Chunsey decided he wasn't cut out to be a police officer. That meant there was a vacancy on the police force. Luckily there wasn't that much crime in Granville that the vacancy could be held open until Matt finished at the academy.

Mom rolled a suitcase to Matt. "I've got the Tahoe loaded down with our wedding dresses, snacks, and these two suitcases will get me through the week. So I'm packed and ready to go myself."

I patted Garrett on the chest. "I wish you could come down on Saturday with Matt."

He gave me a hard look. "You know I can't. This is a big case I'm working on. But at least Nick can ride down with Matt. Hank and I will follow Sunday morning. It's the best I could do."

"I know," I pouted.

"Believe me, I want this case solved just as fast as you do. If I have to listen to Hank give me one more from-one-military-guy-to-another speech about how I should be giving him more information to put into his paper, I'm going to lose it. He definitely takes the Marine mascot to heart."

I laughed. "Hank is exactly like a bulldog. From looks to personality."

Garrett handed me his pie. "I've got to get back to the station. Officer Ryan needs to be relieved. He was nice enough to cover my shift while I had Christmas dinner with you and your family."

I grabbed the plate from him and wolfed down the last two bites while he stood there shaking his head. What can I say…I never let pie go to waste.

"About dang time," Aunt Shirley bellowed loud enough for me to hear her inside the Falcon. I pulled the car to a stop in front of her. "I almost died from exposure out here!"

"I'm on time, you old coot," I said. Okay, I whispered it under my breath. But I still said it, so it counts.

"I can read lips, you ninny!"

I rolled my eyes. *Of course you can.*

Aunt Shirley flung her suitcase in the trunk before I could even get out of the car to help her and then slid into the front next to me. I glanced down and saw a package wrapped in cow wrapping paper sticking out of her huge duffel-bag purse.

There was a long-standing rivalry between Aunt Shirley and Paige regarding cows. It stems from Aunt Shirley once telling Paige my brother would never marry her because, "Why buy the cow when the milk is free." This caused Paige to go hyper insane—an abnormality for Paige. They didn't speak for a long time.

"What's that?" I asked.

Aunt Shirley cackled. "Just a little something I ordered for Paige."

"Is it going to offend her?"

"Probably," Aunt Shirley replied as she buckled her seatbelt.

"Why must you antagonize her?"

14

"I love it," Aunt Shirley said as though it made perfect sense.

I looked out the window and saw an orderly waving me down. His red face had me concerned.

Aunt Shirley slapped me on my arm. "Go, go, go!"

Instinctively, I slammed down on the gas pedal. "What's going on?" I shouted. We fishtailed out of the parking lot, sliding on the slick snow.

"Pfft," Aunt Shirley said and waved her hand at me. "These people have no sense of humor. At arts and crafts today we had to make some lame sculpture out of clay. Everyone was doing a stupid Christmas tree. I decided to spice things up and turn my Christmas tree into a man part. You know the one I'm talking about, right?"

"Aunt Shirley! Geez, they're going to kick you out if you aren't careful."

"What do I care? I don't wanna be there anyhow. It was your boyfriend that put me there."

I refused to rise to her bait. Mainly because to an extent she was right. Garrett and Mom gave Aunt Shirley the choice after she accidentally set her house on fire—and went in public without any pants on—that she could either go to a full-blown nursing home or the assisted living home she was in now.

Pointing the Falcon to the other side of town, I headed to the office to pick up Mindy—leave it to Hank to be working on the newspaper Christmas night.

The office was lit up like a Christmas tree. Which was ironic, seeing as how Hank refused to let us put up a tree or even Christmas lights outside. He said he didn't want people driving by and thinking he ran some froufrou girlie magazine. Yeah, like Hank and *Cosmo* were one in the same.

"Don't forget," Hank said as he chewed on his unlit cigar, "I expect a call in to the office and some type of story every day."

I sighed. "Hank, what on Earth makes you think I'll have something to report on daily?"

He yanked the cigar out of his mouth. "Because I know you two numbskulls." He waved his unlit cigar at Aunt Shirley and me. "Wherever you two go, trouble follows. You're an investigative reporter…go get me an exposé."

I rolled my eyes and headed toward the door. I swear, sometimes I wonder where he gets these outrageous ideas.

"Oh, and if you get my wife caught in the middle of your shenanigans like you did last time…well, let's just say I know how to make people disappear."

Mindy laughed. "Oh, Hank, leave the poor girl alone. No one is scared of your bark anymore."

"Ain't that the truth," Aunt Shirley grumbled.

Speak for yourselves. I just wet myself.

Fearing for my life, I pushed the ladies out the door. "I'll write something daily. I promise."

I felt Hank's glare the whole way to the door. I know Mindy touted his gentleness, but I never saw it.

"Merry Christmas!" I shouted.

"Bah!" Hank turned and went back to the paper.

Once we had Mindy in the car, I had Aunt Shirley text Mom to tell her we were heading out. I figured it would take us a little over four hours since it was still spitting snow.

16

I pulled out of the city limits. "Next stop, South Missouri for some relaxing girl time and a wedding!"

If I only knew then how wrong I'd be.

CHAPTER 3

Cavern Beach is a relatively small town. It has a two-lane highway that goes straight down the middle of town, with numerous businesses scattered along the drag. What makes Cavern Beach different from the other small towns along the lake is that it actually has a small downtown area.

The lake house at Cavern Beach has been in our family for generations. My grandma and grandpa bought the tiny house when they were newlyweds. Years of remodeling projects had turned the once tiny house into a glorious three thousand square foot home spanning two floors. An enormous wooden deck surrounded the house and ran all the way down to our private dock.

In the last ten years, the housing market has exploded in Cavern Beach. Our nearest neighbor, Jim Cleary, is a local contractor. A few years ago he built a gorgeous stone house sixty yards from our lake house. He's a really nice guy, but I rarely see Jim when I'm here because he's so busy.

I made the turn off the main drag onto Highway TT. On this side of town the houses are spread out farther apart. A few minutes later I made a right-hand turn into the driveway we shared with Jim.

"It's about time," Aunt Shirley said. "I've had to pee for the last hour."

I rolled my eyes and turned off the Falcon. Aunt Shirley dashed into the house. "I'll get her suitcase," I told Mindy. "You go on in."

"Want me to send out your mom?" Mindy asked.

"Sure," I said, reaching into the trunk to unload the suitcases. The trunk space in the Falcon was astonishing. You could easily fit at least two dead bodies inside…not that I've tried, of course.

"Hey, sweetheart," Mom kissed me on the cheek. "I've been worried."

"Snow stopped a while back. We've just been driving slow."

Mindy opened the front door as Mom and I carried in the suitcases. I stepped inside the wide foyer, stomping my feet on the welcome mat.

"Bring my suitcase in here," Aunt Shirley called from the archway to my immediate right. "I'm going to stay on this side of the house."

When you first walk into the lake house, the kitchen is on the left, opening up into a great room. Immediately on the right—where Aunt Shirley was staying—were two bedrooms and a shared bathroom. On the other side of the house, was another master bedroom and bathroom. The great room had a staircase leading downstairs that housed three more bedrooms and a bathroom.

I pushed open Aunt Shirley's bedroom door and lifted her suitcase onto the queen-sized bed. "Do you need anything else?"

Aunt Shirley was unloading her purse. "Nope, I'm good."

"What are those?" I exclaimed.

Aunt Shirley scowled at me. "Hush up! We're gonna get caught! These are just a little surprise I have for the bachelorette party."

She handed them to me.

For the first time in my life, I was holding naughty ice trays shaped like…well, like an anatomically correct man. I didn't know there *was* such a thing! "Where did you get these?"

Aunt Shirley scoffed at my innocence. "Off the Internet. You can get anything off the Internet."

I handed the trays back to her. Paige was definitely gonna flip over these…and not in a good way.

"Paige and I are going to run to the grocery store in the morning. Do you wanna go with us?" I asked.

"You betcha! I need to get some booze to do the jello shots. We'll try some out Wednesday night before I decide on which ones to do Friday for the bachelorette party." She twirled the trays in her hand. "I can't *wait* to bust out these lovely beauties."

I shook my head and closed Aunt Shirley's door. I don't know why I'm still shocked at the things she sometimes does.

I walked into the great room. The walls were painted a light crème brûlée. I know this because I spent two days last year painting them. With the natural lighting from the windows it gave the room a warm, cozy feeling.

On the far wall of the living room was a large, sliding glass door that led to the wrap-around deck outside. I crossed the room and walked into the kitchen.

"Is she settled?" Mom asked, handing Mindy a mug of hot tea.

I gave her an incredulous look. "That woman will never be settled."

Mom and Mindy laughed.

"I told her we were going to the grocery store in the morning, and she wants to go to buy some booze."

"Sounds about right," Mindy said.

"What time are Paige and her mom due?" Mom asked.

"I sent her a text about an hour ago, and she said they were just half an hour behind us. So I'm expecting them any minute now."

"I'm looking forward to spending time with Stella and getting this wedding underway," Mom said, filling the teapot with more water. "Do you want tea?"

I wanted something stronger. "Sure."

"How about cinnamon plum tea? It's your favorite."

"Sounds fabulous."

As mom made the tea, I went ahead and took the rest of the suitcases downstairs. There were three bedrooms and a bathroom where Paige's cousin Megan, Paige, Mindy, and I would stay. The room Paige and I were sleeping in had two single beds. When the rest of the group got here—the men—we would have to change rooms around and pull out a few trundle beds, but for now we had plenty of room.

I threw the suitcase on the narrow bed and unpacked quickly. My breath caught when I saw Mom had already hung up my bridesmaid dress. I tentatively reached out to touch the exquisite dress. I wasn't sure how fancy Paige would go since it's just a small, home-style wedding. But she pulled no punches. This was by far the most beautiful dress I'd ever had on my body. It fit like a glove, and I felt like a million bucks wearing it. Of course, I'd only had it on twice, once to try it on and once when the alterations were done...but it was a fairy-tale feeling just the same.

It was a simple, no-frills, pale pink chiffon dress that went all the way to the floor. It had butterfly sleeves and a plunging neckline—not so great for winter. Since we wanted pictures outside, Paige decided we'd both get matching stoles.

I ran my hand down the faux fur. The bright white fur felt soft against the back of my hand. The stole fit across my shoulders and down to my elbows, closing just above my plunging neckline. It would leave a little of my neck and upper chest exposed, but it would keep us warm enough we could take a few pictures outside. We were lucky to be having unseasonably warm weather even though it was snowing a little. Thank you, El Niño.

I was going to be taking all the pre-wedding pictures of Paige. It was my gift to her. The rest of the wedding pictures were going to be taken by Hank.

I pulled out my phone and sent Garrett a text. *"Just checking in. Made it safe."*

I'd just finished hanging up the last of my clothes when I heard the notification from my phone. I looked at Garrett's reply. "Good to know. Try to stay out of trouble this week, Sin."

I ran upstairs to get my tea. As I walked into the kitchen, I heard a car coming down the long driveway. Figuring it was Paige, I ran to the window. But instead of pulling into our circle drive, the headlights veered off and kept on going.

"Jim must be just getting home," Mom said. "He's been working nonstop from what I've heard. Houses are going up all over the lake."

"That's great," I said. "I only got to talk to him for a few minutes when I saw him over the summer. He was busy then, too.

But he still made time to come over and have a beer with us one night."

My mom grew up in this town—and this very house—when both were barely the size of a postage stamp. She went off to college after she graduated high school, which is where she met my dad. They got married, settled down in Granville, and had two kids. He died years ago when I was a little girl, so I never really knew him. Mom decided to stay in Granville…where she spent thirty years teaching at the local elementary school.

I glanced out the window again and watched the taillights disappear. Jim had decided to put a Morton building up a while back. So instead of being able to see the house like we used to be able to do…we now see the back side of a beautiful building made to look like an extension of his house.

For Jim, the Morton building was an extension of his business and offered him more seclusion. For a nosey neighbor like me, it made it impossible to see if he was home or if he had company.

I heard another car. I looked out the window and squealed.

Mindy laughed. "I'm thinking *that* must be Paige and Stella."

I ran to the front door and threw it open. Mom, Mindy, and I slipped on our coats and shoes and helped Paige and her mom carry in their numerous suitcases and Paige's wedding dress. By the time we finished, I was exhausted.

"Wanna grab some tea and unpack?" I asked.

Paige laughed. "Music to my ears."

Mom made up a cup for Paige and we headed downstairs to unpack while Mom and Mindy helped Stella.

"Aunt Shirley already asleep?" Paige asked as she closed our bedroom door with her heel.

"Yep. But she's all excited about going grocery shopping tomorrow to get booze for jello shots," I laughed. "She downloaded recipes from Pinterest for jello shot ideas. She says we're having an impromptu jello shot party Wednesday night to see which ones she wants to serve at your bachelorette party on Friday."

Paige rolled her eyes. "Great, just what I need. Your aunt drunk every day before my wedding."

Paige unfolded her plastic-encased wedding dress from the crook of her elbow. Her wedding dress was almost identical to my chiffon floor-length bridesmaid dress…except it was white. She also had a small band of bling under her breasts for enhancement.

Paige gently touched the sleeve. "I can't believe this is really happening and happening here, at the place we spent our summers. Remember the hours we spent with the town girls laughing and giggling over Matt? This dress and this place is the culmination of all those years planning this marriage."

"Those were good times," I agreed.

Paige hung up her dress. "So you don't think Aunt Shirley will be on her best behavior this week?"

I gave her my best "get real" stare. "You do remember who we're talking about, right?"

Paige sighed. "That's what I'm afraid of."

CHAPTER 4

The ride to the grocery store the next morning was thankfully quiet. Mom and Stella decided to stay back so they could start on the list of food they wanted solely for the day of the wedding. Our job was to pick up supplies and food to last the week. I guess Mom and Stella didn't trust us enough to get food for the wedding…not that I could blame them. I didn't exactly have the cooking gene. That seemed to have slipped through my DNA somehow.

Believe it or not, the grocery store in Cavern Beach is twice the size of the one we have in Granville. Since the towns are comparable in size, I guess the fact Cavern Beach sits on one of the largest lakes in Missouri makes it a necessity.

"Should we split up so this goes faster?" Mindy asked as we walked through the entrance of the store.

"I know what I want," Aunt Shirley said, making a beeline for the liquor department.

I grabbed hold of her sleeve. "Get back here. You're not getting out of shopping that easily."

"What? I'm an old woman. I can't be running around this big ole store getting lots of groceries. My hip will start hurting, my mind will —"

"Forget it," I sighed. "Not worth it, anyway. The three of us will get food, you get your booze."

"Well, if you're sure…" Aunt Shirley took off like her hind end was on fire—so much for her bad hip. She grabbed a cart, plopped her oversized purse down, and practically skipped to the booze aisle.

I shook my head at her childish antics. We quickly divvied up the grocery list and went our separate ways. Since the girls know I don't cook, they decided they'd get the filler stuff, and I'd get the important things like meat. Steak, chicken, fish…that I could handle.

I picked up enough meat to get us through the next four days, then made my way over to the liquor department where I figured Aunt Shirley was still browsing. I should have known browsing was too soft a word. Her cart was filled with bottles of vanilla, orange, cranberry, and peppermint vodka. There was even a bottle of cinnamon whiskey thrown in.

"I'm going to do all holiday jello shots. A cranberry, a peppermint, and a cinnamon!" Aunt Shirley exclaimed with glee.

"That seems like a lot of bottles."

"I'm doing this for two nights," Aunt Shirley said. "I'll make some up tonight and we can have them tomorrow night. Then we can decide what we like, and I can make them up for the bachelorette party on Friday night."

Aunt Shirley was so excited about the prospect of contributing that I didn't want to hurt her feelings. I also had a feeling this could be very dangerous for a group of ladies that didn't typically shoot jello shots.

"There you guys are," Paige said. "Mindy is still getting some items, but I thought I'd try and find you guys and see if we are about ready to check out." Paige peered into Aunt Shirley's cart and shuddered.

"Oh my! Ryli? Paige? Is it really you?"

Paige and I both turned around. My eyes widened when I recognized the face behind the voice. "Julie Crider?"

Julie laughed and nodded as she reached over and hugged us both. She looked good after all these years. She was still a little on the plump side, just like she'd been all throughout middle and high school. But somehow the extra weight worked on her. She had thick, dark hair cut into layers that fell down her back and curled at the ends. Her pouty lips were painted a deep red, and her eye shadow was subtle enough you hardly noticed she had any on. The black slacks and red angora sweater hugged her in all the right places. She looked stunning, even though it was only ten-thirty on a Tuesday morning.

Feeling self-conscious, I smoothed my hands over my hair. I'd hurriedly pulled my hair into a ponytail before leaving the house. The fact I'd just thrown on yoga pants didn't help matters, either. I felt dowdy next to her.

"Yep, it's me," Julie said as she backed away from hugging Paige. "I can't believe this. What are you guys doing here?"

"Paige and Matt are getting married this weekend at the lake house," I said.

Julie squealed. "I always thought you two would end up together. I remember chasing him around the lake when we were kids. This is just so amazing!"

I noticed my Aunt Shirley tapping her toe and giving me a questioning look. "Julie, this is Aunt Shirley. Aunt Shirley, Julie was just one of the many girls Paige and I hung out with during our summers here."

Aunt Shirley stuck her hand out. "Nice to meet you, dear."

Julie shook Aunt Shirley's hand then peered down into her cart. "Looks like you guys are going to be doing some celebrating."

I closed my eyes. Not only had I gotten caught looking like I'd just rolled out of bed, but now Julie was going to think we were a bunch of boozehounds.

"Having a bachelorette party for Paige here on Friday night," Aunt Shirley said. "Why don't you stop by? You girls can catch up."

"Yes!" Paige gushed. "Please say you'll come!"

"That sounds like fun, thanks! You know a couple of the other girls are still in town, right?"

I knew Susie Shoeman was back in town, because she was going to help Paige with her wedding cake. But I didn't realize some of the other girls might still be around. I'd never seen any of them around town when I'd journey down to the lake house.

"They are?" Paige said.

Julie nodded. "Yes, Susie is back in town. She bought a little bakery that's located more downtown."

"She's making our wedding cake," Paige said. "When Matt and I knew we wanted to be married here, we looked up bakeries, and I saw her name. Personally, I couldn't believe she came back here after—"

Paige cut herself off. No one said a word. Well, except for Aunt Shirley.

"After what?" Aunt Shirley demanded.

I peeked over at Julie. She was chewing on her lower lip.

"It happened during the school year, so all the summer kids had gone home," Julie said. "It was our senior year. One night there was a fire, and Susie's parents were trapped inside and died. She and her older sister, Jolene, were able to get out…but her parents didn't make it. There were always rumors and speculation about how the fire started, but nothing could ever be proven."

"What rumors?" Aunt Shirley asked.

Julie looked over her shoulder to make sure no one was listening. Paige and I did the same. Julie leaned in. "Jolene had a long history of trouble. Drugs, boys, drinking…the typical teenage stuff. The last few times, though, since she was technically an adult at nineteen, she ended up doing a couple months in jail. She'd just been released and was back in the home for a day or two when the fire broke out. Earlier that night the police had been called out to the house because of a domestic disturbance. When the police arrived, they realized it was Jolene causing the problem. They left with a warning to her…and that's the last time anyone saw the parents alive. A few hours later the house burned to the ground and Jolene and Susie's parents were dead."

"What happened to Susie and Jolene?" I suddenly felt guilty for never having thought of them after all this time.

"Jolene went crazy after a few years and they committed her to a psychiatric hospital for about five years," Julie said softly. "The truth is, Jolene always blamed me a little for what happened after the fire. I don't know why, but for some reason Jolene thought I told the police she set the fire. And then when Susie came to live with me and my family after the fire so she could finish out her senior year, Jolene really seemed to hate me."

Paige rubbed Julie's arm. "I'm so sorry."

"Thank you." Julie nibbled on her lower lip. "When Jolene finally got out of the mental hospital, she came back here to live.

I'm not sure why. She lives in the trailer park on the outskirts of town, and pretty much does whatever she can to survive, ya know?" Julie's face turned bright red, and I realized exactly what she was saying.

"And what happened to Susie?" Paige asked softly.

"She actually stayed with me and my family until she graduated. By that time, the estate was settled and Susie received the fire settlement and her parents life insurance money. So she just up and moved away. Can't say as I blamed her any. I'd probably want to put this place behind me, too. But then out of the blue last year Susie came back to town and opened up her bakery. It's been doing great, too!"

"I'm so glad I hired her to do my cake," Paige said. "We have an appointment tomorrow morning with her to finalize everything. I can't wait to see her."

"Who else is in town we used to run with?" I asked.

Julie glanced up at the ceiling. "Well, let's see. There's Whitney Lark. She's now a realtor like me. She works for a different office, though. Oh, and Debbie Sanders. Well, Debbie Lancaster now. She married Mark Lancaster, and they have three little kids. I think that's about all of the old gang that's left in town."

Aunt Shirley tapped me with her cart. "You should invite the rest of these girls to the bachelorette party. We'll have plenty of jello shooters."

Like that's the part I'm worried about.

"I have numbers for both Whitney and Debbie. I can give them a call for you if you like," Julie volunteered.

"This will definitely round out my bachelorette party," Paige said.

"Let's do it," I said. "We'll ask Susie tomorrow when we see her for our appointment."

Julie clapped her hands in excitement. "Well, I should run. I actually just dropped by to pick up a bottle of wine for tonight. I have a showing right up until my date tonight, so I figured I'd better run in now and get it."

"So who is this special someone?" I teased.

Julie ducked her head and hid behind her hair for a second. When she looked back up I could see a sparkle in her eyes. "We've been seeing each other for a couple months now. He's *very* busy with his work, so getting together can be kind of difficult. Actually," Julie's breath hitched, "you kinda know him. It's your neighbor, Jim Cleary."

"Jim?" I exclaimed. "That's so cool! I actually haven't talked with him since summer when I was up last."

Julie smiled shyly. "Well, I'd seen him around, of course. And we've had a few deals together with houses, but he's so handsome and charming, and kind of a big-wig right now...I never thought he'd give me a second glance."

"That's so romantic," Paige sighed.

"You're getting married in a few days," Aunt Shirley grumbled. "You think everything's romantic."

Julie laughed. "He's really busy right now, believe it or not. Even winter can't slow him down. Not only are people from Missouri asking him to build their houses out here on the lake, but also people from other states. I'm telling you...he's really going places. People like his easy-going manner and his honesty. Well, that and the fact the man can build amazing houses."

Paige leaned over and hugged her. "I'm so happy for you, Julie. I really am."

Julie laughed. "I'm so glad I ran into you all. I'll definitely call the other girls and invite them over Friday night. Around seven, you think?"

"Sounds great," I said.

"Here's my number, in case you need it." Julie handed me her business card before rushing off to pay for her wine.

"There you guys are," Mindy said as she pulled her cart next to mine.

"You guys done?" Aunt Shirley demanded. "Because my hip is getting stiff from all this standing around."

"Actually, Paige and I have yet to eat breakfast," I said. "I believe that guy over there is handing out wine-infused ice cream. I'm thinking that will be our breakfast."

"I didn't say it was hurting *that* bad," Aunt Shirley said. "I could probably go for some boozy ice cream."

I rolled my eyes. "I had no doubt."

CHAPTER 5

As I pulled the Falcon into our shared driveway, I was surprised to see Jim's truck parked outside his house. I figured as busy as both Mom and Julie said he's been I wouldn't have a chance to say hi.

Aunt Shirley let out a little cat whistle. "Look at that yummy treat."

I looked over to see Jim leaning against his truck, his back to us. Aunt Shirley was ogling his back side.

"Nice," I said sarcastically. I popped the trunk to carry in groceries.

Paige and Mindy laughed as they gathered up sacks and walked into the house. Aunt Shirley was moving more slowly so she could still ogle. I decided the rest of the food could wait and started walking to Jim's truck.

"I understand your deadline," Jim said. "Now listen to me say once again there's nothing I can do right now." He raked his hands through his light brown hair. "My hands are tied. If the materials aren't in, they simply aren't in. I can't produce them out of thin air."

Uh-oh, doesn't sound good.

I didn't want to seem like I was eavesdropping, so I tried hanging back a little. Unfortunately, between the lake and open field, it made for some great acoustics. I started hearing the conversation in my driveway.

Jim turned around. His face went from shock to delight at seeing me. He gave me a tight smile and held up a finger.

He turned his back to me once again. "You'll want to think twice before you threaten me. I'm doing everything I can to keep this project on course. Don't push me." With that he hung up and turned around. "Ryli, long time no see."

Garrett is always complaining I don't know when to just mind my own business, but I had to ask. "Is everything okay?" I gestured toward the phone still in his hand.

"Oh, yeah." He dropped the phone into the front pocket of his flannel shirt. "My secretary, Amber Leigh, got an order mixed up and some of my supplies are a little late. It's no big deal."

"So you have an office here at your home and another one in town?" I asked.

"Yeah. When I first started up, there was no need for an office in town. But now that things have taken off like they have," he pointed to his Morton building, "this is my sanctuary."

He flashed me his pearly whites, and I almost swooned. I know, I know…I have Garrett, but there's something very charismatic about Jim.

We'd taken a small detour on the way back from the grocery store and saw a few of the houses he was building in a new subdivision on the other side of town. They were remarkable…and expensive by the looks of them. I'd say they started out at three hundred fifty thousand dollars just for the basic house.

"What bring you guys down here?" Jim asked. "I've never really known you to do a family Christmas at the lake house."

"That's why I wanted to drop by. We're here for a wedding!"

He laughed. "Yours?"

34

"Heavens no!" I said. "Matt and Paige are finally getting married New Year's Eve."

His grin was contagious and I found myself grinning and tearing up all at the same time. "That's fantastic. Glad it finally happened. I know those two have been circling that fence for a while."

I nodded. "This is true. Anyway, I wanted to let you know all the girls came down early to do wedding prep stuff, and maybe have a little bachelorette party for Paige."

Jim wiggled his eyebrows. "You don't say. You asking me to do some stripping for you?"

I burst out laughing as he moved his hips from side to side. "Well, as tempting as that is, I was just going to invite you over for the wedding."

He placed his hand over his heart. "You wound me. I'll have you know I'm pretty good at bustin' some moves."

"I have no doubt." We stood there a second smiling at each other as snowflakes started falling around us. I decided now was the perfect time to snoop a little. "By the way, I ran into Julie today at the grocery store. Seems she was buying some wine for a date she was having tonight."

Jim's green eyes twinkled back at me. "Is that so? Hmm…wonder who that beauty is seeing?"

I swatted him on the arm. "Bring her, too. She's coming by Friday night for the bachelorette party, but an invitation to the wedding would sound a whole lot better coming from you and not me."

"Is that so?"

"Yep. Proven fact. Girls like to be asked to weddings by guys."

"Then in that case considered her invited," Jim said. "What time?"

"It's pretty relaxed. Probably around two o'clock. I'm hoping the weather stays this nice and I can take pictures outside. So once that's done, we'll start with the ceremony and celebration afterward. Mom and Stella are doing all the cooking and baking, of course. Except for the cake. Susie Shoeman is doing the cake."

Jim nodded his head. "Susie's bakery is amazing. I helped her when she first came to town and wanted to renovate her store. Now I pop in at least once a week for a treat."

"I'm so glad she was able to put her past behind her and come back to town. I can't imagine how difficult it must have been for her."

Jim frowned. "I know it's hard for her. You heard her sister still lives here? Came back to town once she got out of the psychiatric hospital she was in for all those years." He shook his head. "I don't know how Susie holds it together. I'm not one to gossip, but…"

Oh, but I am!

"But what?" I said, hoping for nonchalance.

Jim hesitated. "Well, let's just say Jolene doesn't exactly have the most pristine of reputations. And there's rumors of drugs." Jim stomped his boots on the ground, shaking off some of the snow that had gathered. "That's why I try to go out of my way and make sure I stop by Susie's bakery every chance I get. I want to make sure she feels welcome."

You're a good man, Jim.

36

"I love it when Jim lets us stop by there." A young boy of about eighteen exited Jim's shop carrying two large, yellow halogen work lights. The easy way he carried the heavy objects, it was obvious he didn't need any help.

Jim reached out anyway and helped him set the lights in the back of his truck. "You just like the girl that works there on Saturday mornings," Jim chuckled.

The boy's face turned red. He blew his sandy blonde hair out of his eyes and smiled shyly at me.

"This here is Josh Brighton, my after-school and weekend helper," Jim said.

Josh reached over and shook my hand. "Nice to meet you." He pointed to our house. "That your place over there?"

"Sure is."

"I've always loved the symmetrical deck and natural lighting you get from the windows," Josh said.

I shot Jim a look. What kind of high school kid talks this way?

Jim read my look. "Josh here is strong *and* smart. I'm showing him the ropes on the contractor's side of things. But he'll be leaving in the fall for college. Majoring in architecture," Jim said proudly.

Josh ducked his head and shuffled his feet in the snow, obviously embarrassed by Jim's praise.

Jim slammed the tailgate closed on his truck. "Well, I suppose we should get going. We're hopefully going to finish up on a house tonight before my date. An out-of-town couple who've been pretty anxious for me to finish."

Josh chuckled. "Anxious is putting it mildly."

You don't say?

"And I should get the groceries inside. Aunt Shirley is on a mission to make dozens of jello shots."

Jim threw back his head and laughed. "Your aunt is definitely one of a kind." He looked over at our lake house and grinned. "Speaking of…isn't that her right now?"

Afraid of what I'd see, I slowly turned to look. Suppressing a groan, I watched as an obviously freezing Aunt Shirley sashayed to the end of the wrap-around porch in leopard print high-heeled boots. She looked like she'd just escaped from the zoo. We all pretended not to notice when she slipped on a slick spot of frozen snow, which caused her leopard print mini skirt to ride dangerously high on her thigh. Righting herself, she started waving her hands in a nice friendly manner.

"Jim," Aunt Shirley yelled over coyly. "Good to see you. Don't you look handsome today."

Jim waved back and whispered, "Is your aunt wearing a leopard print mini skirt *and* leopard print high-heeled boots in the dead of winter?"

"Don't ask…just go with it."

Jim chuckled and gave Aunt Shirley a big wave.

CHAPTER 6

"Are you sure you don't want to come with us tomorrow?" I asked. We were all sitting around the kitchen table later that evening, watching Aunt Shirley make her jello shots. I had to admit, not only did they smell delicious, but they looked pretty good, too. I almost couldn't wait until tomorrow night to try them out.

Mindy patted my hand. "No, thanks. I want to help your momma and Stella get ready for the wedding. You guys go and look over the cake. I'm sure you'll want to catch up with your old friend, too. I'm better used here."

"I'm going," Aunt Shirley said from the island barstool. I watched as she carefully poured the cranberry vodka shots into tiny cups. Between the cranberry, cinnamon, and peppermint shooters, the kitchen was beginning to smell a lot like Christmas.

Paige groaned.

"I heard that!" Aunt Shirley said.

Mom chuckled and placed a warm mug of herbal tea in front of me. "What time are you expecting your cousin, Paige?"

"I think Megan should be here around dinnertime. She said her boss is letting her leave work a little early so she doesn't have to drive completely in the dark."

"That's nice of him," my mom said as she delivered the last of the tea to the table. "So here's what I'm thinking as far as timeline. Stella, Mindy, and I will run to the store tomorrow and get the food for the bachelorette party and both the rehearsal and wedding diner. Since it's just a small gathering for the bachelorette party, how about we do finger foods? Maybe some spinach dip, pinwheels, and a veggie tray? And, of course, some chocolate. Then Saturday we'll spend the day prepping for the rehearsal and wedding feast."

I grinned over at Paige. Our moms were great cooks, so anything they made would be better than what we could do. "It sounds wonderful, Janine," Paige said. "Please don't go to too much trouble. I feel horrible you guys are going to be spending most of your days here cooking instead of relaxing and having fun."

Stella patted her daughter's hand. "Honey, we want to do this for you. Believe me, Janine and I are having a great time. We get to bond over cooking and the fact our babies are getting married."

Sniffles and wet eyes popped up around the table.

"Hey, no crying," Aunt Shirley yelped from her area in the kitchen. "There's no crying at bachelorette parties."

"This isn't a bachelorette party," I informed her snippily. "And it's no crying in baseball…not bachelorette parties."

"Whatever," Aunt Shirley huffed. "I should've made some of these beauties up in advance…loosen you girls up!"

Paige got up from the table and went to stand by Aunt Shirley. "They look delicious. Thanks again for doing this."

Aunt Shirley grinned wickedly at her. "Don't thank me until you've seen your wedding-night gift." Aunt Shirley wiggled her bushy eyebrows.

We all laughed at Paige's red face. The poor girl had no idea if Aunt Shirley was serious or not. Me, I knew Aunt Shirley was

40

serious. Whatever the gift was, it was bound to be embarrassing and totally outlandish.

I decided to head downstairs and call Garrett for the night. I hadn't spoken to him or Miss Molly since arriving—just text messages.

I slid my finger over his name and watched as my phone silently dialed his number. Putting the phone to my ear, I bit my lip when it went to voicemail. I left a quick message for him to call me, shut off my light, and turned down the bed.

I heard the bedroom door open and Paige slipped quietly into the room. "I know. I miss you, too. Saturday can't come fast enough. Me, too." There was a huge pause then a giggle. "I'll talk with you tomorrow. I love you so much, Matt. I can't wait to see you Saturday."

When I heard a heavy sigh, I figured Paige was done talking. I rolled over and faced her on her bed. "You two love birds able to survive for a few more days?"

"Barely. Did you talk to Garrett tonight?"

"No. I could only leave a message."

"I'm sure he's fine and totally missing you."

I smiled. "Thanks for being my best friend."

I rolled back over and willed sleep to come. I must have done a good job because I don't remember much after that.

Pulling on my black leggings, I still couldn't believe how unseasonably warm the weather was for December. I hoped it held out until Sunday, the day of the wedding. I yanked on a long, loose flowing red turtleneck and paired it with my equally long black cardigan sweater. I then zipped up my designer black and mocha knee-high boots. They were an expensive splurge, but well worth it.

Twirling in front of the mirror, I decided I looked modern yet causal enough to pick out a wedding cake and chat with an old friend I hadn't seen in nearly ten years.

Today called for a fancier updo than my normal messy bun on top of my head. I'd recently been experimenting with Dutch braiding…and I loved the results. I decided to do a Dutch braid down each side of my head. After pulling at each braided strand and making them bigger and looser, I then pulled the Dutch braids and the rest of my hair on the back of my head into a low ponytail. I only went halfway through on the last loop around the rubber band and then tucked the rest of the hair inside the opposite side of the rubber band. After pulling and loosening the strands, I bobby pinned the mess onto the back of my head.

Super cute if I do say so myself. I was thinking of doing this for the wedding, so I figured today would be a good day to unveil it and see what everyone thought.

As I walked up the stairs into the main center of the house, I couldn't help the fluttering of nerves in my stomach. I knew it was guilt because I was going to see Susie today. After hearing about how bad it was for her after the fire with losing pretty much her entire family, I was anxiety ridden over what to say to an old friend. An old friend I never bothered to contact after hearing the news. I know most people would excuse it and say I was young, but now that I'm older I just feel rotten.

"There you are, sleepyhead," Mom said as I made my way to the kitchen table. Like usual, I was the last to arrive. "I was just getting ready to call down and—oh."

Every head turned to stare at me. "What? I can't be that late!"

"It isn't that," Mom said. "It's your hair. It's absolutely lovely."

I touched it self-consciously. "Do you really think so?"

Paige got up and turned me around so everyone could see the back. "Ryli, it's absolutely divine." Turning me to the side she tentatively touched one of the braids. "I've never seen anything like it. Are you going to wear it like this for the wedding?"

"I was thinking about it. What do you think?"

She squealed and gave me a huge squeeze. "I think it's perfect!" Paige sat back down and fluffed up her choppy layered bob. "I'm just jealous I can't do that to my hair."

"What time are you girls supposed to be at the bakery today?" Stella asked.

"Around two," Paige said as she scooped up the last of her scrambled eggs.

Mom set a plate of eggs, bacon, and toast in front of me. I slathered the eggs and bacon with hot sauce. Twisting off the lid to the boysenberry jam, I spread a generous dollop on my toast. "I was hoping to leave around eleven thirty. Maybe drive around the town, see all the new stores and houses going up. Then maybe get a cup of soup or something for lunch in town before we head over to the bakery."

"Sounds good to me," Paige said.

"Me, too," Aunt Shirley agreed.

Mom gave me a stern look. "I want you to promise to be on your best behavior. Don't go getting into trouble."

I gave her my best "who me" face, but she wasn't buying it. "I'm serious. This is a big deal for Paige. You three have a tendency to run smack dab into trouble when you're together."

I rolled my eyes. "Mom, that was months ago. Believe me, we don't plan on upsetting anyone, much less find a dead body or two while we're here this week, okay. Trust me on this."

Me and my ultra-big mouth.

CHAPTER 7

"I can't believe all the houses that have popped up over the last few years," I said as I eased the Falcon back onto the blacktop road. We'd been driving around for about an hour, looking at all the new commercial and private properties. Over half of them had Jim Cleary's name on the property signs.

"Do you suppose this is how Jim and Julie met?" Paige asked. She was staring at a For Sale sign in the yard of a house that didn't look to be completely finished yet. The listing realtor was Julie.

"I think that's what she said," Aunt Shirley said.

"Do you think they're an odd pairing?" I asked, hoping I didn't sound snobby.

Paige leaned forward from the backseat. "What do you mean?"

I sighed. "I don't know. It's just he's *obviously* rolling in it. I know you can't tell by the way he lives, but you know he has to be doing amazingly well for himself. He's handsome and a bigwig in the community. I've really only seen a few realtor signs with her name on them, so she's probably not that successful. I'd venture to say she didn't leave town like most people did and then came back to settle down. She's probably been here her whole life. I don't know, she's just not what I was expecting a high-profile contractor worth lots of money to go for."

"Julie has always had that thing, though," Paige said quietly from the backseat. "Remember how sweet and innocent she was when we were young. She was so shy because of her size. But there was also something so appealing about her in a nurturing kind of way."

Now I did feel like a heel. Of all the girls we hung out with, Julie was by far the most innocent and sweet. Not at all like Whitney Lark. When Julie mentioned Whitney was still in town, I wanted to ask why in the world Julie even still spoke to her. But obviously she had to if they were both in real estate.

Whitney Lark had been my least favorite local girl to hang with. She was the kind of girl that wasn't from the right side of the tracks, yet made fun of the girls that were. As we got older she'd brag about someday living on the rich side of town—the side my grandparents had built on. Even though my grandparents were far from rich.

Whitney was mean and vindictive, and I was glad I didn't have to be around her all year. I never understood the pull the other girls had to her, but they were all loyal to her.

I nodded. "You're right. Julie's a sweet girl who obviously deserves someone like Jim."

We drove back into town to find a place to eat. After scoping out all the restaurants, we decided on the Cavern Beach Bar and Grill for lunch. With it being winter, a lot of the summer restaurants and bars were closed.

The Cavern Beach Bar and Grill was your typical small-town dive—a brick building located along the main two-lane highway that ran through town. As we walked through the front door, the smells permeating the air made my stomach rumble.

"Hey," a perky teenaged girl called to us with a wave. "I'll be right there." She wove her way between the tables and hurried

46

over. Her fresh-scrubbed face, naturally blonde hair, and tightly toned body screamed high school cheerleader on Christmas break.

"Welcome to Cavern Beach Bar and Grill. My name is Madilynn," she pointed to her nametag on her chest, her ponytail bouncing the whole time. "Is this your first time with us?"

"Yes," I said.

"Well, welcome." Madilynn led us over to a booth by the window. "Best seat in the house for new customers. Everything here is delicious, but I would definitely recommend the baked potato soup with the avocado and bacon grilled cheese sandwich. It's my favorite!"

"That sounds divine," Paige said as we slid into the booth.

"I promise you it is. Darla will be your server, but I can get your drinks for you."

"Water with lemon," Paige and I said at the same time.

"What kind of tequila you got?" Aunt Shirley asked.

I gave Aunt Shirley the death look.

"What?" Aunt Shirley said innocently. "Sign says 'Cavern Beach Bar and Grill' so I'm assuming there's a bar here somewhere."

I continued to stare at her.

Aunt Shirley sighed. "Fine. I'll take water with lemon, too."

Everything on the menu looked delicious, but we all decided on the baked potato soup with the avocado and bacon grilled cheese sandwiches.

After Darla took our order, we pretty much fell into silence, deciding to people watch out the window instead. Since it was winter, pretty much the only people in town were the ones who lived here year round. In the summertime, this place was jumping.

The town came alive with the nightlife. Most people would drive their boats to local restaurants and bars that had popped up all over the channels.

Where we lived, the lake house was still relatively secluded, but at the rate Jim and other contractors were building, pretty soon our little isolated paradise would disappear. Kind of sad when you think about it.

"He's a fool! No one can finish as fast as he wants," an angry voice boomed in the booth behind us. "I'm sorry the homeowners are coming down on him, but he's crazy if he thinks I'm working the holiday weekend to get this house finished for a bunch of rich out-of-towners."

"Yeah. I think this time Jim bit off more than he can chew. I heard they showed up yesterday, and it almost got physical."

"Stupid out-of-towners come here, throwing around money, and they think we're supposed to jump when they say. And dang Jim for jumping through all their hoops…it just makes it harder for us."

A shadow fell over our table. "Here ya go, ladies. Three soups and sandwiches." Darla set our platters down in front of us. "Need anything else?"

"No thanks," we all chimed.

We ate in silence. It was traditional comfort food…and it was amazing.

I tried to listen to see if the guys behind us would dish out any more gossip, but they must have gotten their food, too, because it was silent. I got the feeling Jim was being pulled in a thousand directions with his business.

We paid our tab and piled into the Falcon. We would be a couple minutes early to our appointment, but I didn't think Susie would mind. I wasn't exactly sure where the shop was, just that it was downtown.

"Be on the lookout." I slowly drove the Falcon down a side street that led to the downtown portion of Cavern Beach. While the main drag through town boasted boat shops, real estate offices, and countless restaurants, the downtown was more flower shop, bakery, antiques, and knickknack stores. The police station was also located in the downtown area.

Paige pointed to a building on her right. "There it is." I slowed the Falcon down and turned on my blinker. Luckily there was a parking spot nearby.

The building looked yummy enough to eat. It was painted a pale, creamy yellow…almost like buttercream frosting. The awning had alternating wide stripes of dark pink and light pink all the way around the front. The large storefront window boasted Shoeman Bakery and Treats.

A bell tinkled as I pushed open the door. I was immediately assaulted with whiffs of sugar, chocolate, gingerbread, vanilla, coffee, and myriad other wonderful scents. It was settled…I never wanted to leave here.

I was just about to call out a greeting when I heard voices behind a curtain that led to the back of the bakery.

"Because, Jolene, I have a reputation in this town I'd like to protect, that's why."

"Look, are you gonna give me the money or not?"

"Will you come work for me?"

"Get real, Susie. You don't give me the money, that's no skin off my back. I got other ways to make some quick cash. Hand me my jacket. I'm out of here!"

There was a long pause and I wondered if we should leave and pretend to enter again or what.

"Omigod, is that a syringe?" Susie shouted. "You're using again, aren't you?"

"You ain't my mom, Susie. She died years ago."

Paige and I gasped.

"Don't ever talk about Mom like that again, Jolene!"

Oh, boy! This isn't gonna be good.

Looking over at the wide-eyed stares of both Paige and Aunt Shirley, I decided we'd eavesdropped enough. I coughed loudly. "Hello, is anyone here?"

CHAPTER 8

The curtain was yanked back and out walked a stunning blonde with delicate features and an hourglass figure. Her hair was perfectly coiffed in an elegant Chignon. No messy bun or ponytail for her. Her clothes were just as elegant…and obviously designer. I'd never be able to pull that off while baking. I'm too messy.

"Ryli, Paige, it's good to see after all this time!"

Paige and I ran to her and gave her a hug.

"How long have you been standing here?" Susie asked as she glanced over her shoulder at the curtain.

"Not long," I assured her.

"Yeah. We just walked in," Paige added.

I introduced Aunt Shirley to Susie and tried to surreptitiously peek into the back of the bakery. Was Jolene still there listening to us?

"Let me take care of something in the back real quick," Susie said. "Then we can get down to your cake samples and catch up."

Susie rushed back through the curtain. More whispers, but this time we couldn't hear the conversation. A few seconds later two people came out behind the curtain.

When you hear that drugs can do bad things to your body, believe it. The woman standing before me should have only been a couple years older than me. Instead, she looked to be nearly fifty. Her face was both leathery and wrinkled. Her eyes were sunken in her head, her cheeks were drawn tight, and her face had little pit marks all over it. She was trying to hide behind her stringy, mousy, long brown hair, but was unsuccessful.

"Girls, you remember my sister, Jolene?"

As a teenager, Jolene was always wild and the life of the party…now she was just a sad, pathetic shell of a woman.

"Hi, Jolene," Paige said. "It's nice to see you again"

"Yeah," Jolene mumbled. She scratched her nose and stared out the window.

I could see Susie was about to lose it, so I decided a diversion was necessary.

"I love your shop," I said honestly. "I never want to leave this smell."

Susie laughed. "Thanks. It's one of the things I love most, too."

I was going to ask more questions about the bakery when the bell above the door signaled another customer.

"I swear, that cop even *thinks* of writing me a ticket for my parking job, I'll shove it straight up his—"

"Whitney!" Susie exclaimed. "I have company."

Whitney stopped brushing the light dusting of snow off her raspberry cashmere scarf. It must have started snowing since we entered the bakery. Whitney narrowed her eyes and looked us over from head to toe. I did the same to her.

Her professionally straightened, inverted bob had three different colors of blonde, making it impossible to determine her real hair color. She had a thin, narrow nose and even thinner lips which she'd colored blood red. Her calf-length, double-breasted button down black wool coat reeked of money. So did the fancy designer purse she was carrying.

"Well, as I live and breathe…Ryli Sinclair and Paige Hanson. I heard you two were in town this week. Julie came barging into my office this morning all giddy, like a childish schoolgirl going on and on about you two and a bachelorette party this Friday night." She paused to examine her long fake nails. "I'm fairly certain I'll be busy. I am most Friday nights. But I may be able to stop by if I can find the time."

Don't do us any favors.

"Don't go puttin' yourself out on our account," Aunt Shirley said as she scowled at Whitney. "I'm sure we'll be just fine if you can't make it."

Aunt Shirley…not afraid to tell it how it is!

Whitney let out a loud huff. "I said I'd *try* to make it. And just who are you, again?"

"This is Aunt Shirley," I interjected quickly. I didn't trust what would come out of Aunt Shirley's mouth next. "And we'll be there all night starting at seven. So if you can make it, great. If not, we *totally* understand." I was hoping she'd take my hint and not even bother showing up.

"I gotta split," Jolene said, giving Whitney the evil eye.

I'd totally forgotten Jolene was still in the room. She was that easy to overlook. I suddenly had a fit of conscience. Since she heard us talking about the bachelorette party, did that mean we had to invite her? Or was she so strung out she wouldn't remember what we'd been talking about anyway?

"Jolene, I didn't notice you standing there," Whitney sneered. "You just blend right in, don't you?"

Jolene narrowed her eyes even more at Whitney.

Whitney tossed her head. "You look at little peaked. Maybe you should eat a hamburger on your way home."

There were some serious undercurrents in the room between Jolene and Whitney. They both looked like they could break into a catfight at any moment.

"Please remember what I said," Susie pleaded to Jolene. "I really could use the help."

"Why don't you ask that do-gooder Julie to help you," Jolene mumbled as she headed toward the door.

"That do-gooder took me in and helped me when I needed it. Without her, I don't know what I'd have done."

Jolene snorted as she zipped up her threadbare hoodie and shuffled out the front door. We all silently watched until she disappeared from our sight.

"I just don't know what to do with her," Susie sighed.

"Nothing you can do," Whitney said. "Obviously her stint in the loony bin didn't help her. Even they couldn't fix her. That girl was lost a long time ago…even before the fire killed your parents."

My mouth dropped. I couldn't believe someone could be that crass. I suddenly wanted to ease the pain of Whitney's words. "I was sorry to hear about your parents dying in the fire." I figured we'd better talk about the elephant in the room. I didn't want to start out on the wrong foot and have Susie think we didn't care about what happened to her.

"Yes," Paige agreed. "We were so upset when we heard the news."

A shadow passed over Susie's face. "Thank you. It was such a shock. Then to be displaced like Jolene and I were…well, thankfully Julie's parents took me in for the last few months of our senior year and I could finish up here." Sadness crept into her voice and I felt like kicking myself.

"Well," Whitney said as she hitched the strap of her purse up higher on her shoulder, "I just came in to tell you about the bachelorette party on Friday. But I see you already know."

"I was getting ready to formally invite you," I hurriedly explained to Susie.

Whitney ran her eyes over me. "So you say."

I curled my lip and looked at Paige. I had a sudden urge to rip Whitney's hair out of her head. Obviously my best friend knew that, because she gave me "the look" which meant I couldn't.

"I'm surprised that silly girl didn't run right over here the minute she found out about the party," Whitney scoffed.

"Silly girl?" Paige asked. "You mean Julie? I don't think she's silly at all."

"Please, that girl is beyond ridiculous," Whitney said. "Between her pretend career and current love life…she's so last minute."

I could actually feel my head explode. *Who did this woman think she was?*

"She seemed like a lovely girl to me." Aunt Shirley stared Whitney down.

Whitney looked down her nose at my aunt. "I suppose."

"And goodness knows," Susie chimed in, "her current beau is a catch."

"I don't know what he sees in her," Whitney said. "He's handsome, successful, rich…he could have anyone he wants. Yet he chooses to date her. She's so plain and fat."

"Whitney," Susie admonished. "You know I don't like it when you say those things about Julie. She took me in when no one else could, and she's been one of my biggest supporters since I came back to town. Her and Jim, both. I think it's fabulous they've gotten together."

Whitney's face turned red. That little chastisement shut her up fast. Clutching her designer purse tight to her chest, she tried to unpinch her lips. It took her a few tries, but eventually she managed to get her face under control.

"Although," Susie mused, "I kinda thought he and his secretary had something going on for a while, but I guess not."

"Oh, she wanted to," Whitney assured us. "Everyone knows the only reason she applied for that job was to get close to Jim."

I ignored the gossip and went for fact. "I heard he had an office in town. Where's it located?"

"Yes," Susie nodded. "Over off Sycamore. There's a new section over there that recently went up. It's sandwiched between Luigi's Pizza and Cavern Beach Drycleaners."

"We'll have to take a drive out there soon," I said. "Usually when we come to the lake house we keep to ourselves, rarely come into town. Paige and I were just saying how much everything has grown. It's almost unrecognizable from when we were all kids."

"Indeed," Whitney said. "And on that note, I have a house to show in about thirty minutes." She paused to readjust her scarf and button her coat. "It's a lovely three bedroom, two bath over in a new subdivision that Jim is building. It's quite a steal at two hundred fifty thousand, I must say. My buyers have had me running ragged trying to find the perfect home. But the commission I make will be worth all my hard work."

I barely refrained from rolling my eyes. Guess it's true what they say...money can't buy everything. It obviously can't buy you manners or social skills.

"And I better get these lovely ladies their samples," Susie said, easing the tension in the room. "I hope to see you at the bachelorette party, Whitney."

Whitney shrugged. "We'll see."

Yanking open the door she strolled out of the bakery toward her silver Lexus—which she had parked illegally. She didn't snatch anything off her windshield, so I guess the cop hadn't given her a ticket after all.

Too bad!

CHAPTER 9

Susie threw her hands up in the air. "I know, I know. She's a piece of work. I guess I figured since we were all friends in school, we should still be friends now. But I guess some people change so much, it's hard to remember their good qualities."

"Yep," Aunt Shirley agreed. "Be careful who you trust…the devil was once an angel."

Susie smiled. "Very true."

"I'm just so happy to see you and see how well you're doing for yourself," Paige said. "I still can't believe you own this and that you're going to be making my wedding cake. How did you even make this possible?"

Susie motioned us over to a long counter that had six barstools. We pulled out the chairs and proceeded to watch her haul out samples from a tiny refrigerator.

"After I graduated, I really didn't know what to do. The police were hounding Jolene something fierce…" she trailed off and wiped her eyes. "I don't know if you know this or not, but a lot of people—the police included—thought Jolene had something to do with the fire. But they couldn't prove it. The constant harassment and whispers finally drove Jolene over the edge. About the time she was checked in for the mental hospital, I had received a check from the insurance company. I'd just turned eighteen and needed a clean break. I spent some time down in New Orleans, which is where I started taking cooking classes. I liked it enough, but I still wasn't happy. So I started taking pastry classes, and found I loved baking. I earned a degree and worked for a bakery for many years, honing my skills. Then I decided to come home to try and start over with my own bakery."

She'd set four different samples in front of each of us while she talked. There were two white cakes with filling, a red velvet cake, and a chocolate cake with filling. My mouth watered.

"Did you guys eat a light meal before you came? I suggested it to Paige the last time we spoke."

"Sure did," Aunt Shirley said. "Ate a lovely meal over at Cavern Beach Bar and Grill."

Susie's eyes lit up. "I do love their soup and sandwich combos. They always have a unique blend of flavors you wouldn't normally think about."

Susie gave us each a small glass of water.

"So, I'm going to suggest you start with the lightest cake first," Susie said and pointed to the cake on our far left. "Then work your way to the dark cake. I know most vendors will set out everything separate, but I just went ahead and made the tiny cakes up. We can mix and match anything."

Picking up our forks, we each grabbed the first cake.

"We'll start with the white cake and raspberry filling. It has a buttercream frosting," Susie said.

I bit into the cake and moaned. I was afraid it would be like this for the other cakes, too. Nothing I loved more than sweets.

We all looked at Paige to see her reaction. "I want to hold off on my opinions until the end. This way I don't become biased toward one cake over the others," Paige said.

"Fair enough," Susie said. "Next is the white cake with champagne filling and champagne frosting."

Same reaction for me…glorious.

"Go ahead and drink some water," Susie urged. "It helps to cleanse the palate."

The bell above the door announced a customer. We all turned to stare.

Three women who looked to be in their early thirties came rushing through the door…stomping their feet and muttering about snow. They looked like triplets with their matching coats, trendy boots, and oversized purses. Well, except for the fact they all had different hair color.

Susie excused herself and moved toward the display case. "Good afternoon, ladies. Welcome to my bakery. How can I help you today?"

The leader—Brunette—pushed her way to the front and approached the display case. Her two lackeys—Blondie and Red—trailed closely behind.

"This is your store?" Brunette said as she slowly looked around. "Well, girls, isn't it…quaint."

The way she said quaint made my lips twitch. It was attitudes like these that made locals detest the tourists.

Susie's smiled never left her face. "Thank you. How may I help you?"

I had to give her props…Susie was definitely a professional. I'd have jumped over the counter, slapped them all, then drop kicked their butts out the door.

Which made me sound more and more like Aunt Shirley. I so needed a vacation from her.

"What are those?" Brunette asked.

I listened as Susie ran through the scones and the rest of her items in the display case. Once she was done, Brunette asked for a plain biscotti. As did Blondie.

I barely refrained from rolling my eyes.

Red was the only exception. I liked her. She bent down and pointed inside the display case. "I think I want the cupcake right there."

"The gingerbread cupcake with caramel molasses cream cheese frosting?" Susie asked. "Good choice."

"Do you know how many calories that has in it?" Brunette demanded. "That's like an hour longer on the elliptical."

Red smiled. "I don't care. I want it."

I shook my head at their ridiculous discussion as Susie rang up the Trendies' purchases and then sent them on their merry way. Being nice to rude people was definitely not something I could do every day.

Aunt Shirley grunted. "I'd never be able to do what you do. I wanted to drop kick them on their snotty butts the minute they opened their mouths."

That's it...time to expand my friendship list! Aunt Shirley and I were suddenly sharing a brain.

Susie smiled. "You get used to dealing with difficult people. Comes with the territory."

"Can I ask how you got the red and white icing to do that?" Paige asked, pointing to a cupcake in the display case.

"You mean the swirl on the chocolate peppermint cupcakes? It's actually very easy. You just run a strip of red colorant down two sides of your piping bag, then add the icing. You'll need to pipe out a little before it starts to swirl, but that's it."

Paige's mouth dropped open. "I had no idea! It looks so difficult. It's very pretty."

"Thanks. Creating things with my hands is something I love to do. Okay, how about we get back to tasting some wedding cakes."

"You bet," I said.

"This one is a red velvet." Susie said. "It's one of my favorites." She slapped her hand over her mouth. "Sorry."

Paige smiled at her and bit into the cake.

I picked up the small cake. No need to waste utensils on this one. It had real strawberries and blackberries on top of the ganache frosting. I bit into the cake and closed my eyes, savoring the taste that exploded onto my tongue. Hands down, this was the winner for me.

"Agreed," I said. "I love this one."

Paige hit my arm. "Don't influence me!"

I looked over at Aunt Shirley. She was nodding her head vigorously. Guess it was a winner for her, too.

"This last one is a chocolate cake with raspberry filling."

I bit into it. How in the world Paige was going to be able to choose was a mystery to me. I'd just order them all and have nothing but cake at my wedding.

"So, what do you think?" Susie asked once we'd all eaten our fill.

"I hope I can ask this question," Paige said. "Is there a way for me to order the white cake with raspberry filling, but with the champagne frosting?"

"Of course. You can order whatever you like. I just gave you the samples to experiment with. If you like the champagne frosting, I can do that."

I have to say, I was kind of disappointed. I really liked both the red velvet and chocolate raspberry cake. A white cake? That would never happen at my wedding.

"I think that's what I want to go with," Paige continued.

I refrained from rolling my eyes...barely! But it was her wedding. I guess she could decide for herself.

"White cake," Aunt Shirley scoffed. "Never at my wedding!"

God save me...I was never having a rhetorical thought again. It was like Aunt Shirley could read my mind and was toying with me. No way were we that much alike!

"White cake with raspberry filling and champagne frosting. I can do that. I'll start on it tonight," Susie said. "I still have the design ideas you sent me. Since you decided on white frosting, are you still wanting to go with the dark pink ribbon outlining the base of the cake?"

Paige's face lit up. "Yes, please. Pink will be in the flowers, Ryli's bridesmaid dress, and the ties the guys are wearing."

"And you're still just wanting one round cake? Because I can do a small, two-tiered cake if you like. The base would be about eight inches and the next tier would be only five inches. It's pretty small, but it can still feed about thirty people."

"I didn't realize you could go that small." Paige looked at me. "I think that's what I'd like. Makes it seems more traditional."

I nodded my head in agreement.

"I can also add a little more sparkle to the ribbon if you like. What do you think about adding a cluster of snowflakes made from royal icing with silver dragées in the center, and then attaching them to the front portion of the ribbons? Since there are now going to be two tiers, I think it would look stunning."

Paige nodded her head and wiped tears from her eyes. "I don't know what all that is, but I think it sounds wonderful. You are a life saver."

"I'm glad I could help. Now," Susie said, "what should I bring to the bachelorette party?"

"Oh, nothing!" Paige said. "We didn't invite you so you'd bring something."

Susie chuckled. "I know that. But before you say no, maybe you should know I make a mean Irish Cream mini cupcake. It would be perfect for the bachelorette party."

Paige nodded. "You're right, they'd be perfect."

Paige and Susie finished talking wedding cakes while Aunt Shirley and I walked over to the display case. I was definitely more comfortable looking at sweets than talking wedding cakes. When they finished, Paige and Susie walked over to where we were.

"How about a little treat before you leave? I'd just finished baking it when you came in. It's cooling in the back. Give me a minute." Susie strode behind the curtain, and I practically salivated at the thought of what scrumptious treat she'd bring out for us.

Susie returned seconds later carrying a tray of sliced bread. "I believe I have finally perfected this banana bread. Aunt Shirley, I especially hope you like it. I'm trying to get a market on the health-conscious customers and the older population by offering healthy alternatives. This bread is grain-free, gluten-free, and dairy-free. There are no preservatives in it." I could tell Susie was excited as she practically shoved a piece of the banana bread at us.

Aunt Shirley poked at it with her finger. "At my age, I need all the preservatives I can get!"

CHAPTER 10

"You made good time." Paige hugged Megan hello while I took her suitcases.

"I know," Megan said. "I can't believe how clear the roads are."

"We have supper on the stove," Stella called from the doorway.

"And jello shots for dessert," Aunt Shirley piped up from behind Stella.

We made our way toward the house as headlights veered off toward the Cleary house. "I'll be right back," I told the girls and made my way across the yard. I'm not sure why I suddenly wanted to see Jim—maybe it was all the times his name was mentioned today—but I felt a need to just touch base. I found him cleaning out his truck.

"Well, well…twice in two days. To what do I owe this surprise?"

Laughing, I leaned against the truck bed and watched him unload some tools and take them inside his workshop. I'd never seen so many saws, compressors, nail guns, and cordless drills in my life.

"What the heck is that?" I exclaimed as he pulled out a cordless drill with a two-foot spike.

"This here's an auger bit. Comes in handy when I'm drilling holes in a floor joist." Jim carried the drill and auger bit into his shop. "Hey, why don't you come out of the cold and come in here?"

"I really can't stay. Paige's cousin just got in and we're gonna test out Aunt Shirley's jello shots tonight to see which ones we want for the bachelorette party."

Jim leaned against the doorjamb. "That's awesome. I have to finish some cabinets tonight. I might need to open a window in the shop to get the dust out of the air. I promise not to listen in if I happen to hear you girls."

I laughed. "I appreciate that. The acoustics here make it impossible to keep a secret."

"Sure does," he said, wiping his hands on a rag. "Well, stay warm. I hear we might get another inch of snow tonight."

* * *

"My favorite is the cranberry," Aunt Shirley said. She ran her tongue against the inside of the plastic container, unpopping the jello from the side.

Slurp!

The red jello practically leaped down Aunt Shirley's throat. "Yum!" She smacked her lips together.

I shuddered. It was just too creepy watching her suck up a jello shot like a Hoover sucks up dirt.

Paige sidled up to me and bumped my hip and giggled. "I'm kinda liking the peppermint."

"How many have you had?" I asked her.

Before she could answer, Megan stumbled into us. "About as many as I've had."

"Well, it doesn't help your mom made these cute little matching martini drinks to go along with the shots," Mindy said as she joined our group. She was holding a cranberry jello shot in one hand...and in the other a cranberry martini—or "crantini" as Mom called it. She'd even taken the time to dip cranberries in sugar and string them though toothpicks to add to the cranberry martinis.

They were really good. I'd had two already. Which was why the room was tilting a little...or at least I assumed that was why.

Plop! Plop!

I reached into my jeans and took out my phone. It was a text message from Julie. "Talked with Debbie. Her husband is good with watching the kids Friday night. She'll be at the bachelorette party! Can't wait! Here's her number just in case."

I added Debbie's number to my contacts lists. "Good news," I said to the group. "Julie just texted me that Debbie's going to be able to come Friday night."

Paige let out a yelp. "I'm so glad. It'll be just like old times!"

"I came over to tell you the peppermint martinis were ready." Mindy sucked down a cranberry jello shot and washed it down with a long drink of her cranberry martini. "This was an amazing idea. Aunt Shirley, you outdid yourself."

"I know," Aunt Shirley said, slurping down another red shot. "Wow, those Fireball ones are strong!"

I didn't see this ending well for Aunt Shirley.

"Maybe you should stick with one type for a while," I suggested.

"Maybe you should stick with minding your own business," Aunt Shirley countered back. She reached over and picked up another shot from the tray. She stared me down as she sucked up the shot.

Hiding a smile, I looped arms with Paige and Megan. "Let's go try out these peppermint martinis."

Paige squealed and the three of us sauntered over to where Mom and Stella were making martinis. I picked up the peppermint martini and almost didn't want to drink it...it looked so breathtaking. They had crushed real peppermints into tiny, tiny pieces and rimmed the martini glass with the pieces.

I took a tentative sip. The drink burned my nose and all the way down my throat…but in a good way.

"Mom, Stella, these are amazing," I said as I took another sip. This time I scraped a little of the pieces off in my mouth and chewed on them. *Yep…perfect.*

"Thank you," Stella said. "We concocted the idea watching Aunt Shirley pour the shots. Did the toppers while you girls were sampling wedding cakes today."

"Speaking of the cake," Paige said, "I'm really glad Susie is able to work her magic for us. How perfect is that?"

I turned to Mom. "I was afraid it would be awkward, what with us never speaking to her again after her terrible tragedy, but she really seems to be doing fine. Her bakery is beautiful. You *have* to see it before we leave."

"It really is amazing," Paige agreed. "The way she makes the outside look like a delicious cupcake with her choice of colors…brilliant."

Stella took a drink of her peppermint martini. "I'm just so glad it's working out for you guys. And the fact the girls are going to be coming on Friday night to the bachelorette party is really just the icing on the cake…pun intended!"

We all laughed. I decided a person was declared officially drunk when she laughs at a pun.

"I think I'm going to go sit out on the deck for a few minutes," I announced. "I'm starting to feel a little too woozy."

Mom wrinkled her brow and looked out a window. "Do you think that's such a good idea? It looks like there might still be some flurries."

"I'm going to bundle up really good," I assured her. "Put on my jacket, hat, gloves, scarf, boots…the works. Don't worry."

"Want me to join you?" Paige asked.

I could tell by the pained look on her face she didn't want me to say yes. "No. You stay in here where it's nice and warm."

"Okay," Paige chirped. "I'll make sure this next batch of drinks are just as delicious."

It only took me a few minutes to don my winter attire. Opening the French doors that led to the back deck, I quickly pulled the door shut behind me. I didn't want to hear the girls inside griping about letting the cold in.

The frigid air hit me like a ton of bricks. I breathed in the cold air and my expanding lungs all but froze. Even bundled up like I was, I knew I wouldn't last more than twenty minutes outside.

I walked over to one of the Adirondack chairs that overlooked the lake. This late at night you couldn't see the lake, but I didn't care. I mostly wanted to sober up a little. I slowly lowered my body into the chair, careful not to spill my drink.

Obviously I didn't want to sober up enough that I was willing to let go of my drink.

I could hear Jim's Shop-Vac in the distance. I assumed he was finishing up with the cabinets and cleaning up.

I took out my phone and sent a text to Garrett. *"Girls' night. Trying out Aunt Shirley's jello shots. Fatal."*

His reply was instant. *"Fatal...just like she is."*

I laughed. *"Yep. Can't wait to see you. Miss you."*

"Back at ya, Sin."

I stuffed my phone back inside my pocket and leaned back in the chair. I'd just begun to relax when a noise jolted me out of my daydream of Garrett. Looking behind me, I thought maybe Aunt Shirley or one of the others had joined me outside. There was no one there.

I got up from the chair and walked over to the side of the deck that faced Jim's workshop and house. There was still a light on in his workshop. Figuring that was the noise I heard, I turned back around to go inside the house.

Crash!

"I said...I meant...now!"

I could only make out about every three words. Was Jim arguing with someone again on the phone? This late at night? I wasn't sure what to do.

Crash!

What the heck was he doing over there? Wrapping my scarf tighter around my throat, I tiptoed through our yard and started toward the back of his workshop. Maybe tiptoed was a slight exaggeration, since I had on winter boots. But I tried to be as quiet as possible.

Turning on the flashlight app on my cell phone, I made my way through the freshly fallen snow. I was about twenty yards from the workshop and could hear a little better through the open window. Not wanting to be seen, I crouched down. Dumb I know, since I was out in the open, but it seemed like the thing to do so I wouldn't get caught.

"I can't…done this." I could still only make out a few words. Obviously he'd toned down his yelling.

I couldn't hear the response, but I could tell it was female. I didn't remember seeing headlights come down the driveway tonight, but we'd been pretty busy drinking.

I started to creep forward closer to the window.

"I want you to leave right now and don't come back."

I heard a female's startled cry.

Was he breaking up with Julie? He seemed gaga over her just earlier. What had happened?

"If I have to physically remove you from here," Jim said, "I will."

Not wanting to get caught, I quickly made my way back to my own yard. I picked up my drink I'd left on the deck and tried to slow my breathing back to normal. Taking a small sip, I waited to see headlights. I knew it was too dark to make out a specific car—not that I knew what Julie drove—but I could at least tell when she left.

Whirl!

The sound of a power tool coming from Jim's workshop jolted me. *Had Julie left and I not seen it? No. That was impossible. Had they made up and Julie stayed there to watch him work some more? That had to be it.*

Shrugging, I opened the French doors and went inside. The heat was an instant relief.

"There you are," Paige said. "We were about to go look for you."

I hesitated to say anything about what I'd seen and heard. I didn't want to embarrass Julie by telling everyone, but I also wanted to find out if anyone noticed a car drive down the driveway at any time tonight.

"Mom, Aunt Shirley, everyone, can you guys come here for a minute," I called out.

"What's the matter?" Paige asked.

"I just want to ask something."

Mindy, Mom, Stella, Megan, and Aunt Shirley walked over to where Paige and I were standing. I knew I had to be careful how I worded this…Mom was always worrying about me getting tangled up in things ever since I started discovering dead bodies a couple months ago.

"I was sitting outside on the deck when I heard a noise coming from Jim's workshop. I crept over there to see—"

"Ryli Sinclair," Mom said, "didn't I tell you not to get yourself caught up in something that didn't concern you while you were here?"

I know it's rude, but I ignored her question. "Anyway," I continued, "I couldn't see who he was talking to, but there was definitely a woman in there. He was yelling at her to leave, and he didn't want to ever see her again. All kinds of crazy things."

Paige put her hand over her mouth. "Poor Julie!"

"And?" Aunt Shirley prompted.

"And what?" I asked.

Aunt Shirley rolled her eyes. "And did you see who it was when they drove away?"

"That's just it. I ran back over to our deck, and I waited for the person to leave. Only they never did. The next thing I hear is one of Jim's tools starting up. The only thing I can figure is they made up or something and she stayed there."

Paige blinked back tears. "Do you really think so? I'd hate to think they were breaking up already. Do you think we should call Julie and see if she's okay?"

"I wondered the same thing, but then I'd have to admit I was eavesdropping over at Jim's, and I don't want to do that."

"Did anyone see a car drive into Jim's place tonight?" Aunt Shirley demanded.

"No, no, no!" my mom said, turning to Aunt Shirley. "You guys are *not* going to go butting into things that do not concern you...especially this week. This week is all about Paige!" She ended her tirade by downing the last of her drink.

I was just about to open my big mouth and get myself into a lot of hot water when I looked out the window into the pitch black and saw a car turning on their headlights. The weird thing was they had already pulled out of our shared driveway and gone about twenty yards down the blacktop before they turned on their lights.

I caught Aunt Shirley's eye. She'd noticed it, too. With a small shake of her head, she let me know I was to keep my mouth shut and not say anything.

I almost groaned aloud. I also knew this meant I was probably going to get myself into some hot water pretty soon.

CHAPTER 11

I woke up to pounding on the bedroom door. I rolled over and groaned. The pain of that little movement about made me pee. I tried to open my mouth, but it seemed to be glued shut.

It took me a few seconds to realize the pounding on the door was actually inside my head. I tried to think back to how many drinks and jello shooters I'd had the previous night, but even that was too painful. Thank goodness I'd taken some headache medicine before going to bed. I'd hate to think how I'd feel now if I hadn't.

I heard Paige stirring in her bed. "I hate to think how we're going to feel Saturday morning after the bachelorette party," she croaked.

Perish the thought!

I didn't say anything. Instead I concentrated on making the room not spin. Hoping I had a good hold on everything inside me, I closed my eyes and tentatively sat up.

"It looks like our moms were thinking ahead. They put water next to our beds," Paige whispered.

I slowly turned my head and saw a tall glass of water. Reaching out for it, I drank it in three gulps. I almost felt better.

"I suppose we should be sociable and go upstairs," I said once I could formulate words.

Paige didn't say anything. But she threw back her covers and flung her feet over the side of the bed. Following suit, we both shuffled up the stairs.

Aunt Shirley, Mindy, Stella, and Mom were already sitting around the table eating breakfast and drinking coffee. The table was set with scrambled eggs, cinnamon baked apples, and biscuits.

"I figured you guys could use the biscuits to soak up some of that alcohol," Mom said as she set down plates for us.

It smelled wonderful. "Thanks, Mom." I grabbed two biscuits.

"Is Megan still asleep?" Paige asked.

"I think so," Stella said. "You girls had a late night."

I groaned. She wasn't kidding.

"So what's on our agenda today?" Mindy asked.

I looked over at Paige. As far as I knew we had everything ready to go. The cake was being prepared, the florist was scheduled for tomorrow afternoon, and everyone else was due in Saturday or Sunday.

"I'm just gonna start making more jello shots for the bachelorette party Friday night," Aunt Shirley said as she poured Irish Cream into her coffee.

"Ugh. Are you *still* drinking?" I asked.

Aunt Shirley laughed. "Hair of the dog that bit you, kid." She took a big slurp of her coffee and grinned. "Hair of the dog."

Suppressing a shudder, I took a swallow of my own strong, black coffee. "I think I'm going to go for a walk and look for spots to take wedding pictures. Kinda get an idea of things beforehand."

I pulled my hat over my ears and picked up my sunglasses and camera. Now that I'd had a good breakfast, two more cups of coffee, and another handful of pain reliever, I felt pretty good.

The glare from the fresh snow made me glad I'd grabbed my sunglasses. I headed down to the dock. These days we just kept a pontoon for cruising the lake.

Stepping onto the dock, I felt my body sway with the rhythm of the water. I lifted my camera and snapped a picture of the contrast between the white snow and blue water.

"I know you're here!"

Bang! Bang! Bang!

Startled, I looked up to see what was going on. Unfortunately, all I saw was a blue pickup with the driver's side door still open parked behind Jim's truck.

"You hear me, Cleary? I know you're here because your pickup is parked outside! I told you on the phone the other day that you'd better get my stuff done or I was comin' for you! I'm sick and tired of you putting out-of-towners before locals!"

I made my way up to Jim's house. As I passed by his workshop, I noticed the window was still open. He must have forgotten to close it last night after he finished cleaning up. Boy was he going to regret that when he walked into the shop. It couldn't be more than twenty degrees outside.

I rounded the corner and saw a large man in a dark blue stocking cap banging on Jim's front door.

"Can I help you?" I rudely asked. I didn't know who this man thought he was, but I wasn't going to let him bully my friend.

The big giant whirled in my direction. His eyes narrowed as he looked me over from head to toe. My skin crawled.

"Who're you?" he demanded.

"I live in the house over there," I said and pointed to our place. "You're making enough noise to wake the dead. Figured I better see what all the commotion was about."

The man sneered. "How about you go back inside your house and stay in the kitchen where you belong, and I'll stay right here pounding on this door until this dirtbag opens up!" He turned and started pounding on the front door again.

"Maybe he's not here. You ever think of that?"

The man stopped pounding, turned, and very slowly made his way toward me. It took all my effort not to back up a step, but I wasn't going to let him see I was scared.

Stopping just two feet from me, he leaned down and jabbed me in the chest with his big, beefy finger. Well, he actually jabbed my coat and the three layers of clothing I had on underneath the coat...but the intent was still there.

"Hey, leave my niece alone or I'll rip off your head and feed it to you!"

I laughed.

"That so, old lady?" the vile man sneered. "I'm thinking you two uppity broads need a nice, strong man to put you in your place."

Aunt Shirley whipped out her snub-nose revolver. "I'm thinking your momma should have taught you better manners. Now, get off this property before I blow a hole right through you!"

The man sputtered and practically tripped over his feet as he raced to his truck. Jumping in he closed the door and gunned the truck into reverse, then shot out of the driveway like his tail was on fire.

Aunt Shirley chuckled as she tucked the gun into the back of her elastic-waist jeans. How in the world the gun didn't slide down was beyond me.

"I thought Garrett made you give that gun to him after the last time you pulled it out on someone?" Aunt Shirley had pulled that very gun out on another person back when we were trying to solve the murders a couple months back. Once all the whoopla had died down, and the murder was solved, Garrett had heard that Aunt Shirley had a gun...he told her to hand it over. I had assumed Aunt Shirley had complied. Obviously not.

"I told him the truth. I didn't have it any longer. In fact, I told him to check my apartment...which the little ingrate did!"

"And where exactly was it?" I asked. I knew my aunt well.

My aunt laughed. "I told Old Man Jenkins if he let me stash it in his Oat Bran cereal box I'd let him touch my boobs."

I shook my head and laughed. I'd have given anything to see Garrett's face when he realized he'd been bested by my aunt.

"So what's going on here?" Aunt Shirley asked.

"I don't know. I was down at the dock taking pictures when I heard that guy pounding on Jim's door and yelling. I came up here to see what all the commotion was about."

"I was in the kitchen making up more jello shots when I saw him, too. I had just enough time to grab the gun from my bedroom and run over here."

"I'm thinking we won't mention the gun to Mom or anyone else, okay? No sense getting everyone up in arms."

Aunt Shirley grinned at me. "Good thinking."

I looked around and didn't see any signs of Jim. "I wonder where he is? His truck is still here, and he left the window open in his shop."

"Maybe he worked all night and accidentally fell asleep in there. I'm sure it's heated, so that wouldn't be so bad."

I followed Aunt Shirley to Jim's workshop. The door was shut. Aunt Shirley reached out and pushed the door wide open. He obviously wasn't worried about thieves.

Aunt Shirley was right. The spacious workshop was semi-warm as we stepped inside.

"Hello, Jim?" I called out. "Are you in here?"

No response.

"I'll go look over here," Aunt Shirley said pointing to an area containing lots of lumber and even more saws. "You check over there by the cabinets. Look for clues. Overturned tools, maybe blood."

"Stop!" I cried. I was suddenly afraid to move. I didn't want anything bad to have happened to Jim. Just thinking about what Aunt Shirley was suggesting left me queasy.

"I'm sure it's nothing," Aunt Shirley soothed. "Maybe he left with the person in the car last night. Ya know…went to go get a little hanky panky on." She wiggled her eyebrows in a lewd manner.

I couldn't help but laugh. "I doubt that. Besides, he has a house. Why leave with the person?"

Aunt Shirley sighed. "Just go look you big sissy."

Biting back curse words, I turned and made my way to the cabinetry. I stepped onto a tarp Jim had set down to catch some of the sawdust. The crinkling noise quickened my heartbeat and I felt my pulse jump. Willing myself to calm down, I tiptoed as best I could through the sawdust. Obviously Jim hadn't cleaned up totally like he'd planned.

I stopped in front of the cabinets and looked around. Outside of all the sawdust, everything looked normal.

I'd just turned to make my way back toward Aunt Shirley when I saw a pair of boots sticking out from the side of one of the cabinets.

CHAPTER 12

"Jim," I whispered. My voice seemed unable to register above a whisper. Clearing my throat, I tried again. "Jim, are you okay?"

I peered around the cabinet a little more. My eyes traveled up from his boots to his chest. My breath caught in my lungs, making my chest hurt. Jim was lying on his side, a pool of blood all around him, with the cordless drill and that two-foot auger bit sticking out of his chest.

I cried out and ran over to where he was. I dropped down on my knees and reached down to pull the drill out of his chest. "Don't touch it. He's already dead. Touching it will contaminate the scene more than we already have," Aunt Shirley said.

I looked over at her, ready to yell at her apparent apathy toward my friend, when I noticed she was ghost white and shaking a little.

That was my undoing. I started to cry. I wish I were one of those girls who could find dead bodies and be totally unaffected…but I'm not. This was my third dead body in as many months, but this was even worse. This person I liked. This person was a family friend.

It took all my effort to stand up. When I looked back at Aunt Shirley, she held her arms out to me. I didn't need to be asked twice. I ran to her arms and cried as she held me.

"We're gonna have to call 911 soon," she said when I'd stopped blubbering.

82

"I know."

"You got your phone handy?"

I quietly chuckled. "Of course. Garrett says it's practically attached to my hand at all times." I groaned, thinking of Garrett. "I'm going to have to tell Garrett what's happened, and he's going to blow a gasket over the fact I found another dead body."

Aunt Shirley scoffed. "If he expects to stick around, he better get used to it. It's not like you did it on purpose."

I knew she was right, but I still had a heavy heart. I knew this would put a damper on the wedding. Mom, Paige, and Matt were going to be devastated. Jim was a friend. Nothing was ever going to be the same again.

Looking one last time at Jim, I pulled out my phone and called 911. I gave them the information and hung up. "Should we go tell the others, or what should we do?"

"We need to stay here. Call your Mom and have them bring something warm to drink. I hate to admit it, but I'm about ready to freeze. I just grabbed a light jacket when I went into my bedroom to get the gun and run over here."

I looked sharply at Aunt Shirley. "You don't suppose that guy had something to do with this, do you? Maybe he came out here and killed Jim, then maybe somehow saw me and thought he needed an alibi so he started pounding and making noise thinking I'd come over and investigate?"

Aunt Shirley shook her head. "I don't think so. Jim has been dead awhile. Definitely longer than twenty minutes."

"Oh, right." I sniffed, trying to hold back the tears.

"But it's definitely worth mentioning to the police when they arrive." I could sense Aunt Shirley hesitate, wanting to say something more. It wasn't like her to beat around the bush.

"What else?" I asked.

"I know you aren't going to want to hear this, but we need to think about what we saw and heard last night. You overheard an argument with a female—maybe Julie, maybe not. Then we saw a vehicle sneaking out of the driveway without their lights on. This looks bad for Julie. I know she's your friend, so I'll let you play it however you want, but maybe you just stick with facts. You overheard an argument with a female. You didn't see a car, and you didn't see the person. Let them put the pieces together of who they think it is."

I hadn't even thought about that. Not only was I going to have to answer questions about finding the dead body, but now I was most likely going to have to implicate a lifelong friend. This day officially sucked.

By the time I called Mom, explained what happened, and everyone came over with coffee and a coat for Aunt Shirley, the police and ambulance had arrived. Officer Dillon, a young, fresh-out-of-academy looking boy separated Aunt Shirley and me from everyone else.

Officer Dillon started processing the scene while the EMTs and coroner took care of Jim's body. I put off calling Garrett a little longer. I knew he wasn't going to be happy.

A heavyset, middle-aged man finished giving orders and lumbered our way. Stopping in front of us, he hitched up his pants and just stared at Aunt Shirley and me.

"My name is Chief Taggart. Who found the body?"

I half raised my hand. "I guess I did."

Chief Taggart curled his lip. "You guess? Surely you know. Did you or did you not find the body?"

I was caught off guard. I wasn't used to open hostility from the police.

"Hey," Aunt Shirley said, "how about you take it easy on her. She's still pretty shaken."

Chief Taggart slid his eyes over to Aunt Shirley. "How about you mind your own business and let me do my job."

Aunt Shirley's eyes bugged out and her face turned red. If I didn't step in, someone was going to go to jail…and it wouldn't be Chief Taggart.

"I did," I said quickly. "I discovered the body."

Officer Dillon had joined our small group and was now listening to the questions and answers.

Once again Chief Taggart looked me over. My skin crawled. "And what *exactly* were you doing here? You one of those girls like Good-Time Jo?" He cackled at his own private joke.

"Good-Time Jo?" I asked.

Officer Dillon blushed and shuffled his feet in the snow. He cleared his throat. "I think the Chief is referring to Jolene Shoeman. We've had to pick her up on more than one occasion for soliciting."

Good-Time Jo?

I narrowed my eyes at the sexist jerk. "Do I look like a prostitute?" I held up my hand. "No, never mind. No, I'm not like Jolene Shoeman."

"No, guess you're not," the Chief spit out. "You got a lot more meat on your bones than that strung-out girl. Your hair ain't as stringy and oily as hers, either. Definitely not a user."

I could feel myself shaking with anger. I wanted to make him sing soprano for a while, but I knew I'd be hauled off to jail in a blink of an eye. I guess my face said it all because I felt Aunt Shirley grab my arm.

"I live over there," I said, pointing to our house. "We are here for a wedding. I came over this morning because I heard someone pounding on Jim's door and making threats to him."

Chief Taggart narrowed his eyes at me. "That so? Pretty convenient. Can you identify this man?"

"I can't identify him, but I can describe him and the truck he was driving."

I gave him the description and what I overheard. I could tell the Chief wasn't all that impressed by the way his eyes glazed over.

"That sounds like Larry Blackwell," Officer Dillon said.

"Shut up, boy. I'll do the talking here. Go see if you can't find anything useful."

Officer Dillon shuffled off toward the side of the workshop facing our house. I felt sorry for him. No one should have to endure Chief Idiot as far as I was concerned.

"Anything else?" Taggart demanded.

I looked over at Aunt Shirley. She'd remained silent, but I could tell by the grip on my arm she was getting worked up by this guy, too.

"Only that I overheard an argument last night between Jim and a female. I was sitting on the deck when I heard yelling. I

86

came over and heard Jim say to someone they needed to leave. I left before I had a chance to see who the female was." I felt torn. I wasn't telling on Julie, yet I was making her seem like a suspect.

"And you never saw this person's car or saw them leave?" Taggart asked.

I could tell by his condescending voice he didn't believe me. "No, I didn't. The back half of the Morton building cuts off any visual to Jim's house. Afraid I'd be seen eavesdropping, I decided to turn around and leave. So I just walked back to the house and told everyone what I heard."

Now why had I admitted that?

Again the Chief narrowed his eyes at me. "Dillon," he shouted. Within seconds Officer Dillon came jogging over to us.

"Yes, Chief?" Officer Dillon asked.

"You find any footprints in the snow back there by the side of the shed?"

Officer Dillon's Adam's apple bobbed up and down. "Yes, Chief, I did. Also found footprints leading around to the house and some leading to the workshop. Looks like the same shoe print."

Chief Taggart smiled at me. "That so? How about you show me the bottom of your boots? Bet all the treads will match the ones over here in the blood and sawdust, too."

My pulse raced. *Was he accusing me of murdering Jim?*

"She just told you she was here last night and this morning," Aunt Shirley cut in. "Of course her footprints will be all over this place."

"You know what it sounds like to me?" Chief Taggart asked. "Sounds like you're throwing an awful lot of suspicion on perfectly upstanding citizens like Larry Blackwell and make-believe females."

How could make-believe females be upstanding citizens? What an idiot!

"If I were you, Miss Sinclair, I wouldn't be leaving town just yet. Seems I have me a number one suspect in you." Chief Taggart gave me one last glance.

I momentarily forgot how to breathe.

"Let's go," Taggart snapped at Officer Dillon.

The two men got into the police car and left.

Was I really a suspect?

"Your mom isn't going to like this one bit," Aunt Shirley said gleefully, "but seems to me we have a few days to solve a murder."

CHAPTER 13

"Absolutely not," I said. "Not only will Mom and Paige kill me, but so will Garrett."

"Oh, so you just wanna roll over and go to jail, is that it?" Aunt Shirley asked snidely.

I glared at Aunt Shirley. I knew what she said made sense, but I didn't want to admit it. I didn't want to spend the next few days solving a murder I didn't commit just so I wouldn't go to jail. I wanted to drink and celebrate Paige's wedding to my brother.

"You need to think long and hard, Ryli. We have no time to waste," Aunt Shirley said. "Do you really want Deputy Dipstick and Officer Newbie solving this? Because they looked ready to haul you away right now."

I sighed. I knew she was right. I just didn't want to admit it.

"I think he said his name was Chief Taggart, not Deputy Dipstick," I resigned.

Aunt Shirley snorted. "From where I was standing and what I was hearing…it's one in the same."

I sighed again. "Fine. We do it your way."

I'm so going to regret this!

An hour later we were huddled around the kitchen table drinking hot tea. I still hadn't called Garrett to tell him about discovering Jim, nor had I said anything to Mom about Chief Taggart's covert threat.

"I just can't believe someone would do this to Jim," Mom said as she wiped tears from her eyes. "He was such a nice young man. Always keeping an eye on the house for us while we were gone. Who would do something like this?"

I looked at Aunt Shirley and Paige. I knew they were both thinking what I was thinking. That it could very well be a person we grew up with.

"I told Hank I'd call him today to touch base and say hello," Mindy said as she grabbed her cell phone from her purse.

I groaned. I knew Hank. He could smell a story a mile away. There's no way Mindy was going to be able to keep this a secret. I was definitely gonna have to call Garrett soon. It would be worse if he found out about the body from Hank rather than me.

A few minutes later, Mindy walked back into the kitchen and handed me the phone. "He wants to talk with you."

I took a deep breath and put the phone to my ear. "Yeah?" I said defensively.

Hank chuckled. "I should've known you'd discover a body on your little "girls only" weekend. It's like trouble follows you everywhere."

I could picture him working the unlit cigar back and forth as he talked. "What do you want, Hank? I'm tired and shook up."

"A story," he barked. "I'm assuming you and your wacky aunt are already under suspicion and in need of clearing your name."

How does he do that?

"Maybe, maybe not." I tried to be vague, but obviously failed.

"Just as I thought. I want a story for next week's paper. Get it for me, Sinclair."

"Why in the world would anyone in Granville care if a murder happened here or not?" I asked.

"Don't be an idiot. You and I both know these people will eat it up. Local girl discovers a body, then becomes a suspect in the murder…the papers will fly off the shelf. Especially since it's you, and everyone knows your track record with murders."

I chewed my bottom lip. I knew he had me over a barrel. He's my boss after all, and I *am* a reporter. "Fine. On one condition. I haven't told Garrett about what happened. If you run into him before I get a chance to say something to him, keep your mouth closed. He needs to hear this from me."

"What I wouldn't give to see his face when you tell him. He's going to go ape sh—"

"Just promise me you won't tell!" I interrupted.

"You got it. Oh, and Sinclair, just know if you get my wife involved in any way, I *will* kill you."

I rolled my eyes and handed the phone back to Mindy without saying anything. But inside I was shaking.

Knowing I couldn't put it off any longer, I grabbed my cell phone and headed downstairs to my bedroom to call Garrett. Since I had yet to reach him by phone, I wasn't sure he'd answer this time.

"Hey, Sin. What's up?"

I was totally surprised to hear his voice.

"Not much," I said hesitantly. "You at work?"

There was a brief pause, and then I heard him curse. "What's going on? What've you gotten yourself mixed up in?"

How does he do that?

I choked back tears. "It's not my fault!"

Garrett sighed. "I'm sorry. What's happened?"

I told him everything I could remember…from the argument on the phone the first day I saw Jim, to the guy pounding on the door, to even my suspicion about Julie. I tried skimming over how Aunt Shirley and I found him with the auger sticking out of his heart, but he grilled me on every little detail. I finished the tirade with my run-in with the local Chief, emphasizing he was *nothing* like him…hoping for some brownie points.

"I'm sorry about Jim," Garrett said.

"Thanks," I whispered as I wiped tears from my eyes.

"So, let me guess. Aunt Shirley has you guys trying to solve this case?"

"Did you not hear the part about the Chief of Police telling me not to leave town because I'm his lead suspect?"

Another big sigh. "That's just standard police talk. I highly doubt you're his lead suspect." I could hear Garrett mulling things over. "Why don't I give him a call and see what's going on. One Chief to another."

I instantly felt better. "Thank you."

"How about you thank me by staying out of trouble. I can't go down there right now and bail you out of jail."

My radar went on instant alert. "Why? What's going on back home?"

Garrett chuckled. "Nothing exciting. Still helping Brywood police out with that ring of vandals. Looks like they may be coming our way soon if we don't stop them."

Over the last few weeks a number of houses in the surrounding countryside had been broken into. Brywood was the second town around us to be hit by these thugs. So far they'd stayed away from Granville, but it sounded like it may become a Granville problem soon.

"How's Miss Molly? I miss her something fierce."

"She's hanging in there. She misses you, too. Mostly she just wanders around my house meowing and squinting at me. I think she hates me."

I laughed at the description. "She doesn't hate you. She just misses me."

"She's not the only one that misses you."

The low timbre in his voice made me shiver. What I wouldn't give to have him here so he could hold me.

"I miss you, too," I whispered.

"I'll call the Chief for you when I get a chance."

"Thanks, Garrett. That does make me feel better. And I promise not to get into trouble."

He chuckled. "Yeah, right. You're with Aunt Shirley. Don't make promises you can't keep."

I knew he was right. "I miss you and can't wait to see you on Sunday."

"Back at ya, Sin."

"Do you think we should still go ahead with the bachelorette party after all that's happened?" Paige asked.

Mom placed a bowl of steaming hot stew in front of me while Stella carried over a loaf of crusty French bread.

"I don't want to sound harsh," Aunt Shirley said, "but canceling our plans will not bring Jim back."

Paige sighed. "I know. I just feel yucky thinking about having fun at a time like this."

Mom placed the last bowl of stew on the table then sat down across from me. "Can I weigh in?"

"Please do, Janine." Paige said.

Mom looked at everyone around the table before speaking. "When my husband died, it took me a long time to recover. When the grief finally subsided, I actually struggled with the guilt of wanting to move on. What would people think? Was it too soon to move on? I fretted over other people's reaction instead of doing what was best for my family and myself. I don't want to see that happen here."

I reached over and patted Mom's hand. I had no idea she'd ever struggled with the difficulty of moving on. I turned to look at Paige. "When I told Jim about the wedding, he was so excited for you. He said it was about time."

Megan handed Paige a tissue. "I'm with Ryli and her mom. Don't let this ruin your purpose for being here."

"I know," Paige agreed. "When I told Matt what happened, he pretty much said the same thing. And he and Jim have known each other for years. So if tender-hearted Matt tells me to keep celebrating, I know it's what I should do."

"Being an EMT and fireman, Matt sees tragedy all the time," Stella said. "And soon, when he becomes a police officer, he'll probably see it even more. Believe me, he knows what he's talking about."

94

Aunt Shirley clapped her hands together. "That's the spirit. I'm with everyone else on this. Tragedy happens every day. Don't let it steal your joy."

Paige let out a shaky laugh. "Okay. I guess it's settled. Looks like we're still having a bachelorette party and wedding!"

"That's the spirit, honey," Stella said. "Now, let's try and relax and enjoy our meal."

I'd just taken a bite of the steaming stew when I felt someone kick my leg. I looked up and met Aunt Shirley's eyes. I knew that look. She was planning something. Hoping it wouldn't get us killed, maimed, or otherwise incapacitated before the wedding, I lowered my eyes and dug in. Obviously I was going to need my strength.

When the table had been cleared, and everyone dispersed for the evening, I slipped into Aunt Shirley's room. "What're you thinking?"

"I like the way you get right to the point," Aunt Shirley said.

I sighed. "I figured it's like tearing off a bandage. Let's just get this over with."

Aunt Shirley chuckled. "I think we should sneak over to Jim's and see if we can't find any clues. We'll wait a bit, but if someone does catch us, we can just say we're going for a quick walk to discuss some last-minute party ideas. It's the perfect cover."

"I'm fairly certain there's police tape over the front door of the Morton building."

"There is," Aunt Shirley said. "But trust me. I can get you in."

"I need a drink," I mumbled.

"Right here," Aunt Shirley said, pulling a near-empty bottle of tequila out of her nightstand drawer.

"Of course it is." I walked over and sat next to her on the bed. "Let's have it. I need something to get me through this night."

Two shots later and I was zipping up my jacket and praying Mom wouldn't catch us. I peeked around the corner, into the great room, but it was empty. Motioning for Aunt Shirley, I quietly opened the front door.

"See," Aunt Shirley whispered, "no one will be the wiser."

I knew better. Before the night was over, something catastrophic would happen.

I shut the front door behind me and followed Aunt Shirley to Jim's Morton building. There was still enough moonlight in the night sky that we didn't need a flashlight. And since the police had already seen my footprints earlier in the snow, I wasn't too worried about it.

"While you were on the phone to Garrett, I made a quick run over here. The police locked the door, but they didn't shut the window that was open. That right there should tell you they're idiots."

"So you're suggesting we go inside through the window?" I asked. "How are we going to do that?"

Aunt Shirley didn't say anything until we were under the window. "I'm suggesting *you* go through the window. I can boost you up and you can push it the rest of the way open and climb in. Lucky for you, I've taught you how to pop out screens."

I looked up. It was about a six-foot drop from the window to where we were standing. I weighed my chances of survival if I fell and decided to just get it over with.

96

"Then what do you want me to do?"

Aunt Shirley gave me a disgusted look. "Well, duh, I want you to look for clues."

I sighed. I wasn't exactly sure what that meant. "Okay. Give me your hands."

Aunt Shirley locked her hands together. I put my right foot in her wrinkled hands and on the count of three propelled myself up. Grabbing onto the ledge, I felt around for the soft spot like Aunt Shirley had taught me and yanked hard. The screen popped out. I dropped the screen down and pushed the window all the way up. Luckily, it was wide enough for me to crawl through without ripping the skin off my sides. I looked down at Aunt Shirley to let her know I was ready to hoist myself up the rest of the way. Aunt Shirley's face was red and she was starting to shake.

"Can you push me up a little more?" I asked.

"Can you lose a little weight?" she countered.

My nostrils flared. How dare she criticize my weight. This was all her corny idea, not mine. I was about to give her an ear full when she suddenly pushed her hands up. I shot straight up into the air and fell head first through the window, landing on my back. The air *whooshed* out of my body. Luckily the inside drop was only waist high from the inside.

"You okay in there?" Aunt Shirley asked.

I tried to ignore her. At this point I wanted nothing to do with her, and I cursed myself for letting her talk me into something so stupid.

"Hey, you hear me in there?" she demanded.

I sighed, pushed myself up, and looked around the room. I reached inside my coat pocket and turned on my flashlight app to illuminated the inside of the building.

"I'm fine," I called out.

There were two interior doors. I was betting one led to a bathroom and one to an office. I headed to the door on the right. I skirted around the tarp on the floor and stopped in front of the door. I was suddenly afraid to open it. Twenty-eight year's worth of scary movies were behind that closed door.

I took a deep breath and yanked open the door. Heart pounding nearly out of my chest, I flashed my phone around quickly to make sure the Boogeyman wasn't waiting for me. When nothing grabbed for me, I slowly entered the room.

"What's going on?" Aunt Shirley yelled.

I took in my surroundings.

"Looks like his office," I yelled back. Moving forward I went to Jim's desk. There were so many papers scattered about that I didn't know where to start looking.

Picking up a couple invoices, I noticed there were a lot that Jim had stamped "late notice" on. I recognized Larry Blackwell's name on two of the late notices. Seems ole Larry didn't want to pay his bills. Maybe that's why Jim had stopped doing work for him. But would that be reason enough for Larry to kill Jim? It seemed kind of weak to me.

I'd just flipped through my fourth invoice when I heard Aunt Shirley yelling. "You gotta split. Now!"

Panicked, I dropped the invoices.

I rushed out of the office and back toward the window. "What's going on?" I hollered.

"Not sure," Aunt Shirley cried, "but headlights are coming this way. Get out of there!"

Keeping my phone low to the ground so the light wouldn't give me away, I ran the rest of the way to the open window. The window was waist high from the inside. It would be the drop outside that was the killer. I flung one leg over the ledge of the window and looked down at Aunt Shirley's panicked face. Flinging my other leg over, I teetered on the edge of the windowsill. I suddenly wished my coat was filled with down to help cushion the long fall.

A car door slammed shut. Then another. "No way am I gonna wait to get what I want."

I sucked in my breath. I knew that voice. Willing myself to remain calm, I motioned for Aunt Shirley to move out of my way so I could drop safely to the ground.

"There's tape across the door," a teenaged voice said.

"I don't care! Tear it down."

I pushed myself off the ledge and landed with a jar.

"Ah! I bit my tongue," I hissed. I let my tongue hang down as tears filled my eyes. Hunching over, I motioned for Aunt Shirley to follow me home.

The light in the Morton came on and panic engulfed me. I shot out across the side yard, praying I'd make it home safely without being seen. I'd made it almost to my yard when I realized Aunt Shirley wasn't beside me. I stopped and looked around wildly.

There was just enough light out that I could see her near the tire of Blackwell's truck. I knew it was Blackwell the minute he opened his loud mouth. I put my hands on my knees and breathed deeply. I seriously needed to get into better shape if Aunt Shirley and I were gonna keep doing this kind of crazy stuff.

I stood up and waved Aunt Shirley over. She took off like a rocket across the side yard. For an elderly lady, she could move. I'd venture to say she could outrun me.

I turned and ran the rest of the way up the deck. Plopping down on an Adirondack, I waited until she slid into the chair next to me.

"Whew!" Aunt Shirley said. "That was a close one."

"What were you doing over there," I demanded.

Aunt Shirley smiled. "Just making life difficult for them."

"You know who it was, right?"

"I'd recognize that belligerent voice anywhere."

Me, too. "Why would they risk coming here?"

"Don't know."

"You do realize we accomplished nothing tonight," I said. "I didn't find anything valuable in the building except past due notices to Jim's customers."

Aunt Shirley smiled at me. "We learned Blackwell isn't afraid to cross police tape to get inside Jim's building."

I nodded. "But I'm not sure that really tells us anything."

Aunt Shirley frowned. "Me, either. I wish I knew what he was looking for."

A sudden noise had us looking over at Jim's. It was too dark to see anything clearly, but I could tell Blackwell and the young boy were struggling with a large object.

"Lift your end higher. We still need to get it into the back of the truck," Blackwell snapped. "Now, go make sure that tape is back across the door."

Neither one of us had spoken during the exchange. "Are we just going to let them take stuff from Jim's?" I whispered.

"Don't see how we can stop them," Aunt Shirley replied.

I sighed. I didn't like this one bit.

"Of course, he may not like the consequences," Aunt Shirley chuckled.

"What do you mean?"

"Let's just say pretty soon Blackwell may need to start looking for a new tire."

I gasped and smiled wickedly at her. "What did you do?"

"There might have been an incident involving me and the valve stem core."

We had just turned to go inside when Blackwell suddenly stopped his truck and jumped out. We could hear a lot of cursing and I'm betting a few tire kicks. Looks like it could be a long night for Blackwell and the boy.

I gave Aunt Shirley a high five, quietly made my way downstairs, and sneaked back into my bed. It took a while for my adrenaline-rushed body to calm down enough to sleep. I hoped this was the last of our late-night excursions, but I had a feeling it was just the beginning.

CHAPTER 14

I got up pretty early the next morning and tried calling Julie, but it went straight to voicemail. I texted her and asked her to call or text me immediately.

Deciding to see who was up, I slipped on yoga pants and a sweatshirt and traipsed up the stairs. The living room was nice and bright, and I could see Aunt Shirley standing on the back deck. I went into the kitchen and made a cup of coffee.

Taking my coffee with me to keep my hands warm, I opened the French doors and stepped out into the brisk morning.

"It's so cold that I can see your breath out here even though you aren't talking," I laughed.

Aunt Shirley turned to me, e-cigarette in hand and a guilty look on her face.

"I thought you'd given that stupid thing up!"

Aunt Shirley shrugged. "I've cut back a lot. This is the first time you've seen me smoking, ain't it?

I narrowed my eyes at her. "No. This is the first time I've *caught* you smoking. Big difference."

Aunt Shirley waved her hand in the hair. "Whatever. Same thing."

Not wanting to get into an argument, I counted to five. "Megan, Paige, and I are going into town to the flower shop to check on everything there. We need to get the time narrowed down when the flowers will be available to pick up. Then I was thinking about stopping by the bakery, see if Susie has heard anything more about Jim's murder. You wanna go?"

"Of course. Someone's gotta ask the pertinent questions."

I rolled my eyes and told her she had ten minutes to get out to the car or we'd leave without her.

I went into Mom's room to let her know what we were doing. "We're heading into town to run some errands. We need to see about the flowers and check on the wedding cake. Do you need anything?"

"No. We may run to the grocery store later, but I'm not sure yet. You guys take care. And, Ryli, please don't get into trouble."

I gave Mom a kiss and promised we'd be home later. I didn't promise we wouldn't get into trouble. Mainly because I've learned not to promise things that aren't certain.

Aunt Shirley, Paige, Megan, and I piled into the Falcon and headed into town.

Like Susie's bakery, the flower shop was located in the heart of downtown Cavern Beach. The building was an old, brick building with a solid green awning covering the front of the shop.

"Good morning," a petite, brown-haired woman smiled at us from behind a counter loaded with flowers. "How may I help you?"

"I'm Paige Hanson. You guys are doing the flowers for my wedding on Sunday."

The small woman lit up. "Yes, Ms. Hanson. It's so nice to finally meet you in person. We've done so much talking through e-mails and texts, I feel I already know you." She came over to us and shook our hands. She had a nice, firm grip.

"I was just stopping by," Paige said, "to see what time the flowers will be ready on Sunday."

"I can open the store after church. Say around eleven? Is that soon enough?"

Paige looked at me. "Since you're the one picking them up, is that okay?"

I smiled reassuringly at her. "Of course. I'll already have my hair done, so all I'll have to do is slip on my amazing bridesmaid dress when I get home. Megan, can you help Mom and Stella make sure the flowers get set up where they need to be?"

Megan patted Paige's arm. "Don't worry. I'll help make sure everything is perfect."

"Then I guess eleven works," Paige said.

As Paige and the shop owner finished up, a middle-aged woman with short, curly red hair rushed in, clutching her coat tight against her frail body.

"Good morning." Her weak, nasally voice went straight to my brain.

"Good morning," Aunt Shirley said.

She looked around to find the owner. Seeing her with Paige, Ms. Nasal walked toward them.

"I'll be right with you," the flower shop owner said.

"No hurry, I guess," Ms. Nasal said. "It seems that's the word around these parts, at least."

I lifted a brow and gave Aunt Shirley "the look." Rude people make me angry.

"Are you here for flowers?" Aunt Shirley asked.

"Fake flowers," Ms. Nasal corrected. "I'm tired of sitting around and waiting for our contractor to get out to our place. He was supposed to be done with our house last week. But it seems no one is in a hurry around here. So I decided to come to town and pick up the arrangement for the front room."

"You're building a house?" I asked.

"Yes. Worst decision ever!" Ms. Nasal whined. "Our contractor is constantly not showing up. Just this morning he was supposed to be over, and no surprise, he's a no show!"

My heart dropped to my stomach. While I'm sure there were a lot of contractors in town, I had to wonder about those that didn't show up when they were supposed to.

"Who's your contractor?" I asked Ms. Nasal.

"Jim Cleary," she spat. "I swear, if we weren't so close to finishing, my husband and I would fire him in an instant! He doesn't know how to keep customers happy."

I narrowed my eyes at her. "Jim is dead you heartless witch. Maybe you should watch your—"

Aunt Shirley coughed beside me.

"Dead!" Ms. Nasal cried. "Who's going to finish my house now?"

Obviously realizing I was about to reach over and snatch out the rest of Ms. Nasal's red hair, the flower shop owner rushed over to us. "What can I get for you?" she asked Ms. Nasal.

"A personality would be great," I said.

Aunt Shirley chuckled as she pulled me out of the shop. "I taught you right."

"Can you believe she said that?" I asked incredulously.

"It was horrid," Paige agreed.

"I have to wonder if we shouldn't be looking at either his sub-contractors or unhappy homeowners," Aunt Shirley said. "It seems there were a lot of people unhappy with Jim's speed."

I'm not sure why, but it annoyed me that Jim was suddenly the bad guy. Mainly because he wasn't able to defend himself.

"Well, on a happier note," Paige said, "I totally love my flowers. The bouquets are going to be beautiful. Now for the cake!"

"That means our next stop—"

"Hey, you!" A vise-like grip grabbed hold of my arm and spun me around. There stood Larry Blackwell in all his sexist glory. "I don't appreciate being questioned by the police."

"I don't appreciate being manhandled by a pig. So looks like we're even." I yanked my arm out of his grasp.

Aunt Shirley, Megan, and Paige circled Larry.

He was trapped. Surrounded by a bunch of women who'd rather string him up than look at him.

"Larry…Larry…Larry," Aunt Shirley taunted. "Two truths you should always remember—never turn your back on an ocean wave, and never turn your back on a woman. Both can kill you!"

Blackwell's face turned three different colors. "Now look here." Larry pointed his finger in Aunt Shirley's face. "I don't take kindly to a bunch of *nosey* broads sticking their *noses* in where it don't belong."

"Seems to me it's noses you have a problem with," Aunt Shirley said without missing a beat.

"What the heck are you talking about?" Blackwell sputtered.

We all laughed at Larry's expense.

106

"C'mon girls, let's go," Aunt Shirley said. "Larry…can't say it's been a pleasure."

"Get back here," Larry cried. "I ain't done with you yet."

We left Larry sputtering to himself and headed toward the Falcon.

"I say we eat the goodies at Susie's bakery," Paige said.

"As long as she don't try feeding us that health food crap," Aunt Shirley said. "If she does, I'm out!"

I gave her my best stink eye. "You'll eat whatever she has there. Don't go insulting her."

It only took a few minutes to drive to Susie's bakery. I walked in behind Aunt Shirley and my mouth immediately began watering.

"One second, please," Susie called out from behind the curtain.

"No hurry, Susie. It's just Paige and the rest of us," I yelled out.

A few seconds later the curtain opened and Susie hurried out carrying a tray of scones. Her red puffy eyes left no doubt she'd been crying.

"You're here just before the lunch hour rush," Susie said as she set the scones on the counter.

I glanced at Aunt Shirley. I wanted to be careful how I approached Susie. We'd all changed so much since we were young girls, so I wasn't sure what would set her off.

"These look delicious, dear," Aunt Shirley said as she approached the counter. "Oh, are you okay? You look upset."

Tears filled Susie's eyes. "Of course I'm upset. Jim has been murdered, and my sister is using again. I found her syringes."

Susie covered her face with her hands and sobbed. "I can't believe Jim is dead."

Paige and I ran around the counter and embraced her. "I'm so sorry," Paige said, patting Susie's back. "You must be devastated."

Susie wiped the tears from her face. "I haven't spoken to Julie yet. She's not taking my calls." Tears threatened to spill again. "But I do have comfort in knowing an arrest should be eminent."

My breath caught in my throat. I sent a panicked look to Aunt Shirley. I didn't like the sound of that one bit.

"What do you mean?" I asked.

Susie stepped back from our embrace. "Well, I probably shouldn't tell you this," she said as she pulled a Kleenex from her apron and wiped her eyes, "but Officer Dillon stopped by this morning to get some coffee and scones. He knows Jim stops by…" her voice trailed off and the tears started flowing again. "I'm sorry. I guess I should say he knew Jim *stopped* by here all the time. He said the Chief had already fingered someone. It was just a matter of putting the pieces together."

The spit in my mouth dried up. Had Garrett not called Taggart? Did Chief Taggart really think I had something to do with this?

"Those look mighty good," Aunt Shirley said eyeing the scones.

"Do you want one?" Susie asked.

"Sure do," Aunt Shirley said.

"How about coffee for everyone?" Susie suggested.

Susie busied herself by making coffee. "Are you still going ahead with your bachelorette party tonight?"

This was awkward. "Yes," I said. "We all discussed it, and we think it's the distraction we need. Plus, I'd talked with Jim about it and the wedding, and he was excited. I don't think he'd want us to cancel."

"I understand," Susie said. "And don't worry, I'll still be there with my chocolate goodies. I couldn't sleep last night so I came to the bakery and baked all night. I haven't been home in ages."

Aunt Shirley took a huge bite of her scone. "This is delicious. Much better than that healthy thing you tried to serve me the other day."

My mouth dropped open. She had promised to be on her best behavior!

Susie laughed. "Thanks." She started putting the rest of the scones in the display case next to the éclairs, muffins, donuts, and mini quiches. My mouth watered even more and my stomach grumbled.

"Can I get you guys something, too?" Susie asked.

"Not right now. Maybe before we leave," I said. "Look, I think I need to tell you who it is the Chief is looking at for the murder, and who found Jim's body."

"I tried to ask about that, but Officer Dillon said he couldn't tell me right now who discovered the body. I figured that meant it was the same person they were thinking killed Jim."

My knees went weak, and I stumbled to one of the tables to sit down. Susie rushed over to my side. "Are you okay?"

"It was me," I blurted. "I was the one that found him. Well, Aunt Shirley and I did. But I was the one that actually discovered the body and called the police."

Susie inhaled sharply. "I don't understand."

Megan and Paige walked over to the table and pulled out chairs. Aunt Shirley ambled over to the tray of scones and snatched another.

I sighed. "I heard someone pounding on Jim's door and yelling yesterday morning, so I went over to see what was going on. The guy was angry because Jim was supposed to be working on something for him and Jim never showed up. After he left, Aunt Shirley and I went inside the workshop. That's where I found him."

I didn't tell her *exactly* how I found him, and she didn't ask. She simply nodded her head and cried some more.

"I wish Julie would call me back," Susie said.

Seemed Julie wasn't returning anyone's calls.

"Whitney stopped by a few minutes ago to tell me Julie hasn't been in her real estate office since yesterday. I guess someone from Julie's office called Whitney to tell her this bit of juicy gossip. It seems the police came to Julie's office yesterday to tell her about Jim. She left shortly after the police did. Said she was going home, but no one has been able to reach her."

"How did Whitney seem?" I asked as casually as I could.

"Heartbroken. I think she always thought her and Jim would get together, ya know? Whitney told me that she's already called Amber Leigh over at Jim's office. I guess she's taking it hard, too." Susie's hollow laugh echoed in the bakery. "Why all these women are so upset over a guy who was seeing someone else, I don't know."

"And now it seems I'm the main suspect in Jim's murder," I said.

Susie brow furrowed. "Wait. Why would Chief Taggart think you had *anything* to do with this? That makes no sense."

My thoughts exactly!

"I don't know," I said. "I guess because I told him about what I saw the night before."

Susie looked questioningly at me. I was torn. I didn't want to gossip about Julie or throw suspicion on her, but I also didn't want to go to jail. "Wednesday night I went outside to get some air. It was pretty late and dark outside. I heard yelling down at Jim's workshop, so I walked over to investigate."

Susie gasped. "What did you see?"

"Nothing," I said quickly. "I just heard Jim shouting and so I left before I could see anything."

"Shouting?" Susie asked.

Again, I was torn on what to say.

"Just tell her," Aunt Shirley said with her mouth full of scone.

I looked at Paige and Megan. They both nodded. "I heard him saying stuff like the person should leave, he never wanted to see them again." I didn't say I thought it was Julie.

Susie's mouth dropped. "Omigod. Are you thinking he was fighting with Julie?"

"I didn't say that!" I exclaimed. "I don't know who he was fighting with. I never saw the person. And when they left, I didn't see the vehicle, only that they didn't turn on their headlights until they got out of the driveway."

I knew how bad it sounded for Julie and my heart hurt. "I'm not prepared to say it was Julie."

"Of course not," Susie said hurriedly. "I doubt it was."

Susie folded her hands and took a deep breath. "How was he killed? No, never mind. I don't want to know. I don't want to think of him like that."

I was glad she wasn't going to make me describe the brutal scene again. I wasn't sure I could go through that.

"Do you think…" Susie bit her lip.

"What?" I asked.

"Do you think Julie will admit to being out there and fighting with Jim?"

I looked sharply at Aunt Shirley. I hadn't thought of that. What if Julie denied she was at the workshop fighting with Jim that night? Should we believe her and focus on other female suspects…or does that pretty much make her guilty?

CHAPTER 15

"I say we go pay a visit to this Amber Leigh," Aunt Shirley said.

I'd just turned the Falcon onto Main Street, ready to head home. Of course she'd want to take a detour. Although, I kinda had to agree with her about this Amber Leigh lady.

"I'll plug in the address," Paige said from the backseat.

It only took a second to pull up the directions for Jim's office on my navigation app. I let the soothing voice on the phone tell me where to go.

When we were kids, this section of the town had been all open fields. The only reason to even go on this side of town was to go to Sunbury, a neighboring town.

Now there were streets and houses mixed in with businesses. I turned on Sycamore Drive and drove the recommended distance the lady on the app told me to. And what do you know...my destination was on my right like she said.

"Ryli," Aunt Shirley said, "at some point the girls and I will distract Amber Leigh. You make a break for it and go snoop around Jim's office."

"How about I just ask to use the restroom and have a look around Jim's office?" I countered.

"What if the bathroom is in the front area?" Aunt Shirley argued.

I sighed. "If the bathroom is in the front area, we'll improvise. How's that?"

Aunt Shirley huffed and crossed her arms. "Fine. But I like my way better."

I pulled the Falcon into the large parking lot the three businesses shared. I found parking in front of Jim's office.

"I'm going to text Debbie real quick and see if she's heard from Julie," I said. I scrolled up and got the number Julie left me and sent a quick text.

The four of us got out and headed straight for Jim's office.

Expecting the door to be open, I nearly yanked my arm out of its socket when the door never budged. I jerked repeatedly on it hoping to make enough noise for someone to investigate.

A petite, mid-thirties woman in sweats and sweatshirt shuffled toward the door, hands on hips. Her hair was pulled back in a messy bun, and her face was red and swollen. She stood on the other side of the locked door.

"Open the door," Aunt Shirley yelled.

"Go away. We aren't open today. Or any day for that matter." The woman turned and sashayed away.

The four of us pounded on the door and side windows, yelling for her to open up. Irritated, she stomped back over to the front door, flipped a latch, and yanked open the door. "What part of 'we ain't open' don't you understand?"

I slowly took in her swollen puffy eyes, the grief etched on her face, and immediately felt contrite for harassing her. No matter what her intentions were with Jim, she was obviously grieving.

"Are you Amber Leigh?" I asked. "Jim's secretary?"

She crossed her arms over her chest. "Maybe. Who wants to know?"

114

"I'm Ryli, and this is Aunt Shirley, Paige, and Megan. I live next door to Jim out on the lake."

Amber Leigh stumbled backward as though she'd been slapped. "Omigod. You're the woman that killed Jim! Chief Taggart told me what you did!"

What is that man thinking? Pretty soon I'll have an actual town posse after me!

"I didn't kill him," I assured her.

"That's what *you* say," Amber Leigh said. "Chief Taggart told me differently."

"Chief Taggart's an idiot," Aunt Shirley said. "Ryli didn't kill Jim." Aunt Shirley took a threatening step toward Amber Leigh. While I appreciated the gesture, bullying the woman wasn't going to help make her see I was innocent.

"What do you want?" Amber Leigh demanded.

Paige put a hand on Amber Leigh's arm. "We were wondering how you were holding up? We figured you must be devastated."

"I am," Amber Leigh pouted.

"Jim mentioned you the last time we talked," I added. Of course I left out the part that it was to tell me how she'd messed up an order and now he had some guy ready to pound him. I didn't think that'd win me any points.

Amber Leigh immediately brightened. "He did? I always figured he bragged about me to others. You know, I single-handedly ran this whole operation for him. If it wasn't for me, that wonderful man would have never gotten to where he was."

Delusional much?

"Can I use your restroom?" Aunt Shirley asked.

I shot her a questioning look. What was she up to? That was supposed to be my job.

Amber Leigh narrowed her eyes at Aunt Shirley. I guess she figured an old woman couldn't do much harm because she pointed down the hall.

Paige and Megan tried to distract her with small talk. At first Amber Leigh answered their questions with one-syllable responses, but I could see she was getting restless by the way she kept looking at her watch. Finally after ten minutes and still no Aunt Shirley, she made her way to the hallway.

"I'll get her," I shouted. I was hoping that would alert Aunt Shirley to the fact her ruse was up.

Aunt Shirley came teetering back into the room waiving her hands. "Whew! Don't go in there for a while." Her scrunched nose made me laugh.

Amber Leigh was about to flip out.

"Jim seemed like he was doing great with the business," I said.

Amber Leigh sighed. "He was such a dreamer…while I was the down-to-earth captain that ran this ship. We made a great team. It was only a matter of time before we took the next step and merged our business and personal life."

"I thought he was seeing Julie," Aunt Shirley said.

I heard Megan almost lose it behind me. Amber Leigh obviously didn't know Aunt Shirley was purposely baiting her.

"Well," Amber Leigh said, "you didn't hear this from me, but Jim was getting ready to dump Julie and move on. He'd finally realized the great team we made."

Was this true or was she just trying to make herself look good? Could Jim have really been ready to dump Julie and that's what the fight was about the night he was murdered?

"What about Josh?" I asked. "How's he holding up?"

Amber Leigh rolled her eyes. "That boy is such a pain. The way he followed Jim around like a little lost puppy was so pathetic. Jim was usually good about tolerating him, but I could tell he was annoyed a lot."

"What a witch," Aunt Shirley mumbled behind her hand.

"Excuse me?" Amber Leigh said.

"I said...I have an itch," Aunt Shirley said, pretending to scratch her nose.

"Do you have Josh's address?" I asked.

"Why?" Amber Leigh demanded.

"We just want to make sure he's doing okay," Paige said softly.

"Well, I'm not supposed to give out phone numbers or addresses, but I guess I can get it for you."

A few seconds later, address in hand, we all piled into the Falcon. I glanced down at my phone and noticed I'd gotten a text while inside Jim's office. It was from Debbie. I quickly read the text.

"Seems Debbie hasn't heard from Julie, either," I informed the girls. "I'm beginning to really get worried about Julie. I say we cover all the bases. Before we head over to Josh's place, we go over to Julie's work first. Maybe she's either checked in or someone there knows where she may be."

Julie's real estate office was a brick building situated on one of the busier streets in town. The large sign out front read *Paulsen Real Estate*. The business shared a parking lot with a Dollar General next door.

"Welcome to Paulsen Real Estate." A buxom brunette with a wide fake grin greeted us from behind a long counter. "How may I help you?"

She was between twenty-five and forty. With Botox so popular nowadays, sometimes it's hard to tell. I'm not sure why, but to me she looked like a Botox user. I peered a little closer at her chest and saw her name was Tammi. "Well, Tammi, we're friends of Julie's. We haven't been able to reach her. Do you happen to know where she might be today?"

"Oh, isn't it just awful?" Tammi wailed. She lifted a tissue and dabbed delicately at the edge of each eye. "We're all still in shock. We worked a lot with Cleary Construction over the years. Jim was such a nice man."

"Yes, he was," I said. "But we're worried about Julie. No one is able to reach her."

Looking over each shoulder to make sure no one was around, Tammi leaned in toward us. "You didn't hear this from me, but I heard the police are questioning her." By the gleam in her eye, I'd say this wasn't the first time she'd repeated this little bit of news. In fact, I'd bet my left foot Tammi was the person that called Whitney to tell her about Julie not coming in to work.

"Well, I've met your Chief," I said. "I'm sure accusing everyone is his way."

Tammi tilted her head. I could tell by the puzzled look on her face she had no idea Chief Taggart was an idiot. "What do you mean?"

I looked over at Aunt Shirley. She gave me a little nod. "I mean, he doesn't seem all that competent. Instead of conducting a thorough investigation, he seems ready to pin this on anyone— even me—without proof."

Tammi's nostril's flared and her lower lip quivered. "How *dare* you accuse my uncle of shoddy police work! If he's looking at you for the murder, then I'd say you're the murderer." She jumped up from her chair and pointed her perfectly French-manicured hand to the door. "I think you'd better leave. Now!"

The four of us shuffled quickly out the door.

"Well, that went well," Aunt Shirley grumbled.

"Did we learn anything?" Paige asked.

I laughed. "We sure did. We learned Cavern Beach is like Granville. It's a small town and everyone is pretty much related to everyone."

"True," Aunt Shirley agreed. "But we also learned Chief Taggart is looking pretty hard at Julie. Why else would he demand her presence at the police station instead of questioning her at her house after such a tragedy? Maybe he did hear what you said about having overheard an argument with a woman."

This didn't sit well with me. I felt like I was betraying Julie. Just because I overheard an argument didn't mean I was convinced it was Julie. Jim seemed to be fighting with a lot of people lately over business. While I admit the argument with the female in his shop sounded more personal, I wasn't willing to risk a friend going to jail on this assertion.

We started toward the Falcon when Aunt Shirley grabbed my arm. "I need to run into the dollar store real quick. Gotta pick up something."

"Give me the keys," Paige said. "Megan and I will warm up the car while you two run in."

Handing her my keys, Aunt Shirley and I bustled inside the store. The layout was pretty much the same as it was in Granville. I followed Aunt Shirley as she made her way to the cosmetics area. "What're you getting?"

Aunt Shirley stopped in front of the dentures section and picked up a bottle of Fixodent. "My dentures keep falling out. I'll tell you what, ever since they took Rigident off the market, life for denture wearers has never been the same."

She snagged two packages of Fixodent off the shelf and shoved them in my hands. I started walking toward the checkout line when Aunt Shirley suddenly tapped me on the shoulder.

"Hey, I forgot something. I'll be right there. Go ahead and get in line."

There was only one guy behind the row of registers. That's usually the way it is at our dollar store, too. He looked to be around twenty, carrot-red hair, freckles galore, and skinny as a pole. I set the two boxes of Fixodent on the conveyer belt and stood in line behind a young woman in medical scrubs and orthopedic shoes.

By the time our purchases were next up, Aunt Shirley was standing next to me. A nice-looking man in a business suit fell in line behind us.

"My grandma likes this brand," Red said as he rang up the Fixodent.

"It's the only thing that works for me now that they've taken Rigident off the market. Best stuff there ever was," Aunt Shirley reminisced.

Suddenly out of nowhere another box came flying past me, landing on the conveyer. I looked down at the box. *Trojan: Ribbed for His and Her Pleasure.*

I turned and glared at Aunt Shirley…at the same time wishing the world would open up and swallow me whole. I heard a chuckle behind us. The businessman dressed in the snazzy suit and holding a Coke was staring at the box. I accidentally made eye contact with him, and for a brief moment I thought I was going to faint.

Feeling my face heat up, I ducked my head down and prayed the poor cashier boy would not die of embarrassment—much like I wanted to do.

"Hey, cool," Red said. "I like these ones, too!"

I jerked my head up so fast that I heard my neck crack.

Another chuckle from end-of-the-line Coke guy.

"You can't even—you can't have—why do you—never mind." I was shaking so hard I couldn't even get the words out.

Red was gently placing the condoms in the same bag as the Fixodent. Unholy images of Aunt Shirley and Old Man Jenkins flashed through my head. Images that will haunt me until the day I die.

"Just give him the money," I moaned.

"Simmer down," Aunt Shirley snapped. "It's not like no one here's never seen a box of condoms. I should be getting an award for practicing safe sex!"

A full-blown laugh from end-of-the-line Coke guy. Grabbing the plastic bag, I practically ran out of the store...cursing Aunt Shirley the whole time.

CHAPTER 16

Josh Brighton lived on the same side of town as Julie's work, so it didn't take long to locate his house. There were about fifteen houses in this newer subdivision, and each house led to a private dock. The Brighton house was a spacious, two-story brick home.

Pulling the Falcon into the driveway, the four of us hopped out and walked toward the front door. I rang the bell and waited for an answer.

The door was yanked open by a teenage girl, probably sixteen, with long curly hair comprised of a shocking array of blues, greens, and purples. She looked like Rainbow Brite.

"Nice hair!"

"It's like a rainbow exploded in your hair!"

"Super cool!"

We oohhed and aahhed over the girl's hair. Aunt Shirley was bold enough to wrap a curl around her finger.

"I so need to do this to my hair," Aunt Shirley said wistfully. "How did you do it?"

"Kool-Aid," the bubble-gum popping girl said. "I can do it for you if you want."

Aunt Shirley turned to Paige. "I'm gonna do this. I know you have a wedding, but..."

Paige laughed. "I think it's fabulous."

"Sweet! C'mon in. My name is Brianna," the girl said as she led us into the house.

"We're looking for Josh," I said. "I'm friends with Jim, and we wanted to check and see how he's doing."

"Aren't you guys sweet," Brianna said. "He's totally bummed. Go on into the kitchen and I'll yell for him to come down."

The four of us walked down the hallway toward the back of the house.

"He said he'd be down in a second," Brianna said as she skipped back into the kitchen. "Can I get you guys something to drink?"

"No thanks," I said. "We just came from Susie's bakery where we had scones and coffee."

"Oh, I love her store. She has the best stuff," Brianna said as she proceeded to mix various Kool-Aid packets with conditioner in small bowls. "Of course, Josh likes it because Carrie works there on Saturday mornings."

"Who's Carrie?" Aunt Shirley asked.

"Carrie is a senior, too. She's worked for Susie since she opened. She's totally cool and popular," Brianna said. "Josh really doesn't stand a chance, but he tries."

"Shut up, brat," Josh said good-naturedly as he strolled into the kitchen. He watched his sister mix for a few seconds before shaking his head and grabbing a drink out of the refrigerator. "Which one of you brave ladies is gonna be her guinea pig today?"

Aunt Shirley's hand shot up. "I am. I'm getting me some purple and pink hair."

"Your hair will really take the color, too," Brianna assured Aunt Shirley. "It's already a light color."

"I was hoping to talk to you about Jim," I said to Josh.

Josh took a long drink, his eyes never leaving mine. "Why?"

"I want to get a better feel for this whole murder. It just doesn't make sense. I was hoping you had some thoughts or ideas about who would want to harm Jim."

Josh's eyes began to water, and I was afraid he was going to lose it. Not wanting to embarrass him further, I pretended to be interested in what Brianna was doing.

Brianna put a large towel over Aunt Shirley's shoulders and had Megan tearing off sections of aluminum foil. She showed Paige how to take a small section of hair and add the pink to the top portion, then blend in the purple at the bottom section, then wrap it in the foil.

"And how long does she keep these in her hair?" Paige asked.

"I'd say a couple hours," Brianna said. "Were you going somewhere after this?"

"Nope," Aunt Shirley said. "And even if I was, I've looked crazier, so it's no big deal."

I heard Megan chuckle as she handed Brianna the last of the foil she'd torn off the roll.

"Let's sit down at the table," Josh said quietly.

Pulling the chair out I sat and watched him move the cap from his drink across the table back and forth in front of him. "I'm not sure what I can help you with. I already told Chief Taggart everything I know, too. And that is I don't know as much as I thought I did about Jim, because I never thought he could make someone mad enough to kill him. He was a really nice guy, ya know?"

"You already talked with Chief Taggart?" I asked. I had to admit, I was a little shocked. Taggart looked like he moved at a snail's pace, yet suddenly he was questioning the whole town—mainly about me and my motive to kill.

Josh chewed on his lower lip. "Yes. He came to the house yesterday morning to tell me what'd happened. He also told me you were the one that discovered the body. He asked me lots of questions about you, but since I'd just met you the one time, I couldn't tell him anything." Josh waved his hand in front of him. "Not that I think you did anything. I honestly don't."

Well, you'd be the only one in this town right now that thought that.

Josh shifted in his seat. "I wasn't supposed to meet up with Jim until about ten that morning. He wanted me to sleep in and relax. It's my Christmas vacation, and Jim didn't want me to work too hard."

"That was awful nice of him, seeing as how half the town was breathing down his neck," Aunt Shirley said from her barstool in the kitchen.

Josh smiled half-heartedly. "That's the thing about Jim. He didn't care. He went at his own pace, regardless of the amount of people breathing down his neck. He always said quality work took quality time."

Josh looked out the window, and I could see he was fighting the urge to cry. I knew I needed to redirect him or I'd never get anything pertinent out of him. "Do you know Larry Blackwell?"

Josh nodded. "We are doing work—or I guess we *were* doing work for him. Now that Jim's dead, I don't know what will happen to Jim's business or the houses we were in the middle of doing."

"And I'm sorry for that," I said. "I heard Jim arguing on the phone with someone, and I think it was Larry. Then I witnessed Larry at Jim's house the day I discovered his body. He was pounding on Jim's door, threatening him if Jim didn't finish his job." I watched Josh's body language very carefully. "Do you think Larry could have killed Jim? Could he have gotten mad enough at Jim to take his life?"

Josh chuckled. "No way. Larry's all talk. He's always been a little hotheaded like that. But I've never known him to be violent. Like I said, I can't imagine anyone doing this."

While I envied his naivety, I knew he couldn't be more wrong. I once thought no one I knew could ever kill another person…until that person tried to kill me. As much as I hated to admit it, I wouldn't be all that surprised if it was Julie. Upset, yes. But not surprised.

Josh cleared his throat and leaned forward. "If you are looking at arguments and people that might be mad at Jim, there *was* something that happened last Saturday."

"Last Saturday? Like right before Christmas?" I asked.

"Yeah. Jim and I stopped by Susie's bakery," Josh blushed. "You know, because she has really good stuff."

I smiled encouragingly at him, not wanting him to stop because he was embarrassed. "Yes, they do."

Josh's eyes fell to the table then back at me. "Well, as Jim and I were walking out the front door to go to Jim's truck, we heard some fighting in the alleyway."

"Who was it?" Aunt Shirley called out.

I hadn't been aware Aunt Shirley was listening, but I guess I shouldn't be surprised. I looked over at her and tried not to laugh.

She looked like a silver octopus with the randomly placed foils popping out all over her head.

"It was Whitney Lark and Jolene Shoeman. I'm not sure what they were fighting about. I just heard Whitney tell Jolene that a person like her didn't need to be hanging around Susie, and that Jolene should have just stayed away and never come back to town because everyone knew she was the one that killed her parents in the fire."

"How does Jim fit into this?" I asked.

"Jim motions me to follow him into the alley where Whitney and Jolene were fighting. When they see us, they suddenly change. Whitney gets all nice again, and Jolene tries to sneak off."

This kid better hurry up before I pull out my hair.

"So Jim walks up to them to see what's going on, and Whitney tried to pretend that we heard wrong. That they weren't fighting. Jim told Whitney he heard what she said to Jolene about her parents, and that—well, he kinda got mad at Whitney and told her she needed to grow up and mind her own business. That the last thing Susie needed was for her customers to see two grown women fighting in an alley. And that if Whitney was really Susie's friend she'd just keep her mouth shut."

I smiled. Boy would I have loved to have seen that.

"Well, that is interesting," I said, "but I'm not sure if that would cause either one of them to kill Jim."

Josh cleared his throat. "I haven't finished. So after Jim told Whitney to grow up and keep her mouth shut, Whitney went all crazy on Jim, telling him to mind his own business or she'd put him *out* of business. He should just run on home to his…" Josh stopped talking and shifted in his seat. "He just needed to run on home to his fat, unsuccessful girlfriend."

I could tell he wasn't saying something. "And?"

"And the truth is, if anyone was going to be killing that day, it would be Jim killing Whitney. He was so mad at her. I'd never seen him so angry."

Funny how Whitney left that part out when she was talking about Jim in the bakery. Of course, that also accounts for the evil eyes between Whitney and Jolene.

"What about Jolene?"

Josh shuddered. "It was super gross. After Whitney and Jim finished bickering, Jolene slides up to Jim and puts her arms around him. Telling him if he ever gets tired of Julie that *she* could keep him warm at night."

I crinkled my nose. "Gross," I agreed.

Josh let out a shaky laugh. "Yeah, Jim all but threw her off him. We practically took off running out of there. It was super creepy and scary."

I thought about what Josh told us. Even I had to admit it was a huge stretch to think because of that incident either Whitney or Jolene would kill Jim. But, I wanted to keep my options open. So for now, Larry, Whitney, and Jolene were all prime suspects...along with Julie.

"Okay, you're done," Brianna announced. "You can rinse your hair tonight. It should be nice and bold by then."

"Perfect. My Kool-Aid hair can match the jello shots I'm serving tonight," Aunt Shirley said.

CHAPTER 17

"I think I'm gonna try calling Julie one more time," I said to Paige as I tossed down the magazine I'd been reading. It was mid-afternoon and we were lounging on our beds trying to rest up for the party later.

Mom was still trying to calm down from her near heart attack when she saw Aunt Shirley's octopus-foiled hair. To say she was raging mad might be an understatement. I hadn't seen Aunt Shirley since she slunk to her room to hide from Mom's wrath.

"Good idea," Paige said.

I picked up my cell phone. I didn't want to give up on Julie. I wanted to believe there was a reason why she was ducking my calls.

"Hello?"

"Omigod, Julie? I'm so glad you picked up."

Silence.

"I wasn't sure if I was going to or not," Julie admitted.

"How are you?" I asked. "I mean, I know that sounds lame, but we've been so worried."

Julie sighed. "I guess I'm okay. I mean, I'm totally shocked and heartbroken, but…" I heard sobbing on the other end.

"Oh, Julie. Please don't cry," I murmured. "Come over tonight. I really think you need to be with friends."

Julie continued sniffling for a few seconds. "I don't know, Ryli. I just don't know if I have the strength. I've spent most of the day at the police station—"

"Did that horrible Chief Taggart haul you in?"

Paige flung her legs over the side of her bed and leaned forward to hear better. I pulled the phone away from my ear so she could listen in.

"Yes. He made me go down to the station and drilled me for about two hours. I really don't know anything, Ryli. I swear."

More sobbing.

I put the phone closer to my ear. "Please come over tonight. Even if it's just to be surrounded by people who love you."

More sniffling. "Maybe you're right. I don't know how much fun I'll be, but maybe I need to get out. I can hardly breathe here. I feel like I'm suffocating."

"Great! We'll see you tonight. And Julie, don't worry, we'll get this sorted out soon."

"You both look beautiful," Mom said as Paige and I walked up the stairs and into the kitchen later that night.

Paige had on a black and white maxi skirt with an off-the-shoulder black sweater. The sweater was tight and fit her curves nicely. I had on my signature outfit of black stretch pants, oversized tunic, and designer boots.

"Thanks," I said, kissing Mom on the cheek. "You look nice, too."

Mom had on black dress pants and a long-sleeve, button down, hunter green blouse. Her long, blonde hair was caught at the nape of her neck in a decorative barrette.

Before Mom could say anything, Aunt Shirley swaggered into the room.

"What about me?" Aunt Shirley demanded.

I took in her new purple and pink hair, fuchsia pants, and see-through white blouse and shuddered.

"Love the hair. But, seriously, what the heck are you wearing?" I asked.

Aunt Shirley looked down at her top. I could see her old-lady bra through the sheer material. "What? I was told it's all the rage."

I snorted. "It's all the rage for twenty-year-old girls with perky boobs."

Paige grabbed my arm. "*Please* tell me you know what she's wearing to the wedding!"

Mom laughed. "Don't worry, dear. I took care of it."

Aunt Shirley huffed. "She's got me in a nun outfit!"

"Oh, thank God," Paige whispered.

"Aunt Shirley," my mom admonished, "a black skirt paired with a cream sweater is not a nun's habit."

"Yeah, well it ain't my habit to wear, either!" Aunt Shirley cackled and slapped her hands together gleefully.

I rolled my eyes at her sad joke. Okay, it *was* kind of funny, but I didn't want to give her a big head by admitting it.

Headlights flooded the dimly lit living room. "Someone's here," I sang.

Paige and I rushed to the door to greet our first visitor. A curvy woman carrying a party bag and two bottles of champagne stepped out of a minivan.

"I hear there's a party going on!" she cried as she ran up the steps and into our arms.

Debbie's super-short, red spiky hair was sticking out in all directions, and I'm pretty sure one of her spikes poked me in the eye. Her heavy makeup failed to hide the dark circles underneath her eyes.

"I heard you have three kids!" Paige exclaimed.

Debbie laughed. "Yep. Nine, six, and two."

That explained the dark circles under the eyes. Guess three kids and a husband will do that to you.

"It's been a crazy ride," Debbie said. "Want to see pictures?"

"Of course," Paige said.

We all gathered in the living room as Debbie showed off her crew. They were a cute family with two girls and a boy.

"Now that we got the boy," Debbie laughed, "we're done."

"What's Mark up to?" I asked.

Debbie put her pictures away. "He's selling boats at Cavern Beach Marine Motors. He makes a good enough living that I'm able to stay home full time and take care of the kids."

I wasn't sure if that was a good thing or a bad thing. Three kids seemed ridiculously overwhelming.

"Both my girls are in dance and tumbling, so that keeps us pretty busy most nights. And Trevor, the baby, just keeps me busy getting into everything he can."

"It's a great age," my mom said as she set a tray of food down on the coffee table in front of us.

Plop! Plop!

I looked at my cell phone. It was a message from Garrett. "How's it going? You 3 sheets to the wind yet?"

I laughed out loud and sent a text back. "Nope. Just starting. Miss u, can't wait to see u."

133

"Same here, Sin. Be safe tonight."

"You, too. Don't let Matt do anything too crazy. I'll call you tomorrow. Tell Miss Molly I love her."

I put my cell phone back in my pocket. "Garrett's getting ready to go pick up Matt for his bachelor party."

"I'm not sure I want to know that," Paige said.

I rolled my eyes. "Please. A handful of guys staying in Granville to drink. How much trouble can they get into?" I tried to sound flippant, but I had to admit, a little part of me worried. I'd heard about some pretty racy bachelor stories before.

"Speaking of drinking…what're we having?" Aunt Shirley sashayed over to the bar and started setting up glasses.

I looked at my watch. I figured Susie and Julie would arrive soon. I'd never heard back from Whitney, so I had no idea if she was coming.

"I think I'll start with champagne," Megan said.

"Perfect," Aunt Shirley said. "I froze some champagne yesterday. I'll just go get the ice cube trays."

I let out a groan. I'd hoped she'd forgotten about those.

"What trays?" Paige asked.

I didn't say a word. No way was I going to have Paige yelling at me.

Aunt Shirley rushed back in a few seconds later with her naughty trays. "Look what I got!"

The girls all squealed in excitement. I frowned and suddenly wondered when had I become the stick in the mud? Aunt Shirley poured champagne into a glass and topped it off with raspberries and strawberries…and a little something extra. I thought for sure

Paige would be mortified at the male body part floating in the drinks.

"I'll have one," I said.

"Me, too," everyone else chimed in.

Aunt Shirley busied herself pouring drinks. Every time she moved, I was treated to a not-so-nice view of her sagging skin and boobs.

"Are you seriously wearing that hideous blouse all night?" I asked.

"It's for the stripper," Aunt Shirley said. "I want him to know I'm available."

Champagne shot out of Paige's mouth and nose. "Please tell me she's not serious. You guys didn't do something as vulgar as hire a stripper, did you?"

I laughed at her expression. "Not that I know of. But I can't say what Aunt Shirley did."

Paige glared at Aunt Shirley.

Aunt Shirley pretended not to notice.

Headlights filled the room and saved Aunt Shirley and Paige from duking it out right there on the living room floor. I looked out the window and saw a car pull into the circle drive. "I bet that's either Susie or Julie."

Paige and I met Susie at the front door. She had her arms full carrying a gift bag and two plastic containers. Figuring the containers had the Irish Cream cupcakes in them, I snatched the containers. I couldn't wait to try them.

"Susie, it's so good to see you again," Mom said as we set the sweets on the kitchen counter.

The two women embraced. "Thanks, Mrs. Sinclair. I'm happy to be here tonight. Takes my mind off of things."

I felt a stab in my heart. I was horrified at the tears welling up in my eyes. This was supposed to be a joyous occasion. "Have you heard from Whitney or Julie?" I asked.

"Whitney said she'd be here after she finished showing a house," Susie said. "But I never could reach Julie."

"I spoke to Whitney around three o'clock today," I said. "She said she was going to come. She needed to get out of the house."

"Good!" Susie exclaimed. "I've been so worried about her."

The buzzer on the stove sounded.

"That's the spinach dip," Stella announced. "Why don't you girls go into the living room and relax."

"That's quite a blouse you have there," Susie said diplomatically to Aunt Shirley.

Aunt Shirley beamed. "Thanks! I'm hoping to stand out when the stripper gets here."

Susie lifted an eyebrow at me.

I shook my head. "There's no stripper."

"We'll see," Aunt Shirley said mysteriously.

CHAPTER 18

We sat around and drank more champagne and caught up on old times. Mindy and Megan were troopers, laughing and listening to our childhood stories.

A car pulled into the driveway and I hopped up, hoping it was Julie.

A few minutes later Whitney strolled into the living room. "Hope I'm not too late. I just finished showing a house on Market Street. I figured I'd drop by while I had some time."

"I'm glad you made it," Paige said. "We were just catching up on old times. Filling Mindy and Megan in on our shenanigans."

Whitney sniffed. "I don't reminisce much about those times."

An awkward silence filled the room.

"You want something to drink?" Aunt Shirley asked.

"I'll have vodka over ice," Whitney said.

Aunt Shirley frowned. "We don't have anything hard like that. We have champagne."

Whitney sighed. "That's fine."

We spent the next half hour scarfing down food, drinking, and laughing. It was nice to be able to relax and not think about the murder…or how I was a suspect.

"Susie, these boozy cupcakes are amazing," Megan said.

"I concur," Mindy added. "I must have the recipe if you'll share it."

Susie smiled, "You bet."

I pulled out my phone and texted Julie. "Where r u? Missing you. Please stop by tonight."

I looked over at Whitney. She'd just taken her blood and was getting ready to inject herself with insulin.

Worried, I hurried over to her. "Are you okay?"

"I'm fine. Lots of sugar in the food and drinks. I just need to balance my sugar level. That's why I mainly stick to harder liquors. But since you don't seem to have any, I guess I'll just have to stick myself all night."

I swear my eyes crossed. This woman was so passive-aggressive it wasn't funny.

"I'm curious," I said. "Have you spoken to Julie? Or maybe Jolene?"

I waited to see the reaction I'd get when I mentioned Jolene. Sure enough, Whitney took the bait.

"I haven't spoken to either one of them. Why would I? It's not like we hang out or anything."

"Yeah, I heard about the fight you had with Jolene in the alleyway last Saturday. Seems you and Jim were overheard bickering at each other."

Whitney narrowed her eyes at me. "Don't be believing everything you hear from that idiot Josh."

I didn't bat an eye at her description of Josh. "Why were you so mad at Jolene?"

"Not that it's any of your business," Whitney hissed so she wouldn't be overheard, "but Jolene's way of life is bound to hurt Susie's business. I hate seeing Susie be the butt end of gossip yet again. It was hard on her when her parents were killed and Jolene was the main suspect. Now that Susie is trying to get her life back together, Jolene's constant drug use and arrests for soliciting are going to hurt Susie all over again."

"So it was out of the kindness of your heart you threatened Jolene? And then insulted Jim by talking trash about Julie?"

Whitney glared at me. "What's your point? You think I killed Jim? You're an even bigger idiot than your joke of an aunt."

I felt my blood boil. "You'd do well to never speak of Aunt Shirley like that again."

I stomped over to the bar and snatched up a jello shot. I tilted my head back and caught movement out of the corner of my eye. Whitney was hunched over her phone typing rapidly.

"I should be going," Whitney suddenly announced, slipping the phone into her pocket. "I have an early morning tomorrow. I have a buyer wanting to see a house on Montgomery Street and then a house on Sage."

I wasn't completely sad to see her leave. Old friend or not, she was lucky I didn't deck her with the jab about Aunt Shirley.

It only took a few minutes for us to shove her out the door. Good riddance to her and her negativity.

"Should we open gifts?" Mom asked once Whitney had left.

I looked at Paige. "I don't know. Should we wait for Julie or…"

"I think you should open them now," Stella said. "With all Julie has been through, she probably hasn't gone to the store to buy anything. No sense making her feel uncomfortable when she gets here."

"Okay, bring the gifts on!" Paige said.

Mom and Stella went to gather the gifts while Aunt Shirley served another round of drinks.

I sat next to Paige, totally intending to take notes on what gifts she got. It only took three seconds for me to realize I was too tipsy to take notes.

"I've got you covered," Mom whispered as she placed the last gift down.

I thanked Mom as Paige went to town opening her gifts. She mostly got cookware from Mom and Stella. No surprise there. Even Susie and Debbie got Paige cookware. Guess that made sense seeing as how one owned a bakery and the other had to cook for nearly a half dozen people.

Mindy got Paige a basket filled with lotions, candles, and other good smelly stuff for her honeymoon. Megan bought her a beautiful white negligée with a matching wrapper. And I bought her a case of her favorite wine…for her honeymoon and many nights to follow.

"I'm hoping for a niece or nephew soon," I joked.

It wasn't until Aunt Shirley jumped up from her chair that we realized her gift wasn't on the table.

"Silly me," Aunt Shirley exclaimed. "I must have left it in my room."

We all looked at each other warily. This couldn't be good.

Aunt Shirley returned a few minutes later with her gift. When I saw the gift bag, I burst out laughing. It was the large black and white bag designed to look like a cow. I'd completely forgotten about seeing that package.

"Here ya go," Aunt Shirley said as she thrust the large cow print gift bag at Paige.

Paige groaned. "I'm almost afraid to look inside."

"I found it on the Internet," Aunt Shirley said as she took another drink of her champagne.

Paige reached inside the bag and pulled out a cow print, babydoll negligée with matching cow-print panties. It was the most atrocious thing I'd ever seen.

"Omigod!" Paige laughed. "I love it!"

I whipped my head around to look at her. Had she suddenly gone insane? It was absolutely appalling. I mean, it was a cow print negligée with matching panties! Obviously Paige was ridiculously drunk.

"What?" Paige said, look at me. "I think it's cute. I can't wait to wear it."

"Let's have another round of drinks," Aunt Shirley said.

I was working on my third or fourth drink of the night when I remembered I should be keeping an eye out for Julie. I checked my watch again. She should have been at the house an hour ago.

"Still no Julie?" Susie said.

"No. I want to call her, but I don't want to pester her, either."

"Let's dance!" Mindy shouted as she turned up the music on my iPod speaker.

Mindy gyrated her hips and beckoned my mom to dance. All things considered, this was turning into a fun night.

Headlights flashed across the room as a car pulled into the driveway. "I hope that's Julie," I said as I walked to the front door.

I was just getting ready to open the door when loud banging startled me. "This is the police. Open the door immediately."

I looked over my shoulder, but the music from the iPod was so loud no one else had heard.

I quickly opened the door. Standing on the front porch was Chief Taggart. He was dressed in tight polyester blue pants, light blue shirt, and one hand was resting on his holster.

"Officer Clark," Chief Taggart barked over his shoulder, never once taking his eyes off me, "go inside and start taking names of individuals here. I'll be in in a second."

"Yes, sir," a nervous-looking boy said. He looked to be around Officer Dillon's age...or even younger if that was possible. He shuffled past me, trying hard to look like he wasn't scared to death.

"What's going on?" I demanded. "You can't just come in here and barge into our house without a warrant."

Chief Taggart sneered and leaned into my face. "Oh, I can get a warrant in a heartbeat. Just know if I have to go that route, I'll make sure this house is turned up on its side. No way you could have a wedding here in two days."

I closed my eyes. Better to let him ask questions, but Garrett was definitely going to hear about this. Chief Taggart was undeniably abusing his power.

"What's happened?" I suddenly got a bad feeling about Julie. Maybe there was a reason she wasn't answering her phone. "Is it Julie?"

Chief Taggart's mouth twisted in a sneer. "Funny how that's the first place you go. Like you know something already. You're not playing your hand very smart."

"Shut up and tell me what's happened!"

Chief Taggart grabbed my arm. "Now listen here. I'll—"

A sudden commotion had us both looking into the living room.

142

"I *knew* a stripper would show! Let me guess, our music was too loud and now you need to arrest us all?" Aunt Shirley practically screamed. "Whoo hoo…take it off, big boy. Take it off!"

My mouth dropped open. Aunt Shirley was gyrated her hips suggestively at Officer Clark, waving a dollar bill in his face. The poor kid couldn't help but stare at her saggy boobs as she shimmied and shook for all she was worth. It wasn't until Aunt Shirley turned around and tried to twerk that I finally snapped out of it.

"Stop!" I yelled, running into the living room. "Paige, turn off the music. This is serious, Aunt Shirley. He's a real cop."

Paige shut off the iPod. The whole room looked scared. "What's going on, Ryli?" Paige demanded. "It's not Matt or Garrett, is it?" I could see she was going to start crying any minute.

"I'm not sure what it is," I said. "Chief Taggart was getting ready to tell me."

Chief Taggart took his sweet time looking us all up and down. He then walked in front of the bar, taking into account the amount of alcohol and empty bottles and glasses around the room.

"Looks like we got a nice party going on," he said condescendingly. "Makes me wonder what kind of women could party it up knowing one of their friends is dead. Brutally murdered."

"What are you talking about?"

"Omigod, who's dead?"

"What's going on?"

Everyone started speaking at once.

Chief Taggart held up his hand. "We just got back from processing the scene over at Julie Crider's house. She's been murdered."

Susie dropped her drink and started to fall. Mom caught her before she went all the way to the ground and led her to an empty chair.

"What do you mean coming in here and announcing something like that you pompous jerk!" Aunt Shirley said.

Chief Taggart narrowed his eyes at Aunt Shirley. "Watch it, old lady, or I'll arrest you for indecent exposure and assaulting a police officer. Cover yourself up! You look ridiculous. And what is with that hair?"

I wrapped my arms around Aunt Shirley. Physically holding her back was the only way to keep her from decking him. And we didn't need to make an extra trip to the police station to bail her out.

"Obviously you ladies aren't in any shape to drive to the station tonight and answer questions," Chief Taggart said. "So I'll be expecting to see *you* and *you* bright and early at the station. You understand me?"

He had pointed to Susie and me. We nodded our heads simultaneously, too frightened to speak.

Someone had killed Julie? Why?

Chief Taggart turned on his heel and motioned for Officer Clark to follow. I slammed the door shut behind them, too shaken to care how it looked.

Mom was rubbing Susie's back when I walked back into the living room.

144

"Why us?" a weeping Susie asked. "Did we do something wrong?"

I felt a twinge of pity for her. Not only had she lost her parents to a fire, had a meth addict for a sister, but now she'd lost a new friend in Jim, and a childhood friend in Julie.

"I don't know," I said honestly. "I think because we both knew Jim and Julie. They probably just want to question us."

"I'm sorry about the spilled drink," Susie said to Mom. "I don't know what happened. I just started shaking and lost my balance."

Mom patted her arm. "You were just shocked is all. We all are. I'm thinking we put on a pot of coffee and call it a night."

"I'll get the coffee started," Stella said as she hurried into the kitchen.

"Do you think you'll be able to drive home tonight?" Mindy said chewing her lip nervously.

Susie smiled at her. "Thanks for worrying about me. I've actually only had two glasses the whole night. I knew I had to drive home, so I was pacing myself."

I looked down at the glass I'd picked up after slamming the door on the police officers. I *think* this was my third or fourth. I was definitely not pacing myself.

"What about you, Debbie?" Mindy asked. "You okay to drive home?"

Debbie had been quietly sitting on the couch throughout the exchange. She'd already cried through four Kleenexes. "I'm fine to drive home. I'm just in shock. I can't believe this!" She started sobbing again.

Paige went over and sat on the couch next to her. "Is there anything we can do for you?"

Debbie shook her head and wiped again at her eyes and nose. "No. I'm going to call Mark real quick and let him know what's going on, and that I'll be home shortly."

"Of course," Paige said.

Stella handed Susie a cup of coffee. "I hate the thought of you going home alone after all this."

Susie blew on the coffee then took a tentative sip. "Oh, I won't go home. I'll go to the bakery. It's where I've spent the last few nights, anyway. When I'm sad or worried, I just bake and bake. I can't help it."

"I'm not sure that's safe," Aunt Shirley said. "Let me just remind you all that there's a killer on the loose. He's already killed two people."

Susie took another drink of the coffee. "I hadn't thought of that."

"Maybe you should just stay here," Paige urged.

Susie stood up and handed her mug to Mom. "I appreciate the concern, but I'd feel safer at my bakery. Plus, I need to try and get ahold of Jolene. I haven't spoken with her at all today. She keeps avoiding my texts. And, I need to get started on a wedding cake."

"I just don't know how I can think about a wedding at a time like this," Paige said.

"Oh Paige," Stella said. "Please don't say that!"

"It's true," Paige insisted.

Knowing how tenderhearted Paige was, I knew she'd think something silly like that. "Paige, nothing is going to take the joy

146

away from your wedding, you hear me? Nothing. No matter what, you and Matt are going to be married on Sunday. No…matter…what."

Paige looked over at me and smiled. "I understand."

I just wished she looked like she believed it.

CHAPTER 19

After Susie and Debbie left, we wasted no time cleaning up the mess and turning in. While Paige was getting ready for bed and brushing her teeth, I called Garrett to tell him about Julie's murder.

The bachelor party was still going strong, so Garrett had to take my call in a different room. I could tell he was worried, especially when I mentioned Chief Taggart demanding my presence at the police station in the morning.

"I don't understand," Garrett said. "Why is he fixated on you?"

"I honestly don't know. For some reason, he thinks I either know something or had something to do with the murders. I don't even know yet how Julie died. He just said she was brutally murdered."

Garrett sighed. "I wish I could head down with Matt and Nick tomorrow, but I honestly can't get away right now. I'm lucky Officer Ryan is covering for me Sunday. It's been crazy here."

"I understand," I said. I learned a couple months back that a cop, especially a Chief, doesn't have banker's hours. I've learned to take what I can when I can.

I heard the faucet shut off. "Paige is almost done getting ready for bed, and I don't want to upset her any more than she already is. I better turn in."

"I wish I was there right now to help you through this."

My heart leaped. "Me, too. Sunday can't come fast enough."

148

"Call me tomorrow after you meet with Taggart."

"Will do. You about finished with your party?"

Garrett chuckled. "Wouldn't you like to know?"

I rolled my eyes. "Whatever. Just be safe."

"Night, Sin."

I hung up and stared at my cell phone. I wasn't sure I was ready to tackle Taggart in the morning, but I didn't really have a choice.

"So what are we thinking?" I asked Paige once we were snuggled in bed that night.

Paige leaned up on her elbow and looked at me. The nightlight from the bathroom illuminated our bedroom just enough for me to see her in the dark.

"I'm thinking I'm scared," Paige said. "I think someone is killing people we know, and we don't have any idea who it is."

I kept my mouth shut. I didn't want to tell her I had a few suspects in mind. I knew she'd just worrying about me, and what Aunt Shirley and I were planning on doing.

"We've been best friends since elementary," Paige said. "I can tell you're up to something. What gives?"

I guess I just thought I was going to keep my mouth shut. "I'm not exactly sure. Aunt Shirley and I have been—"

Paige's groan cut me off.

"Well, you asked!" I exclaimed.

"I know, I know. Go ahead."

I turned on my back, mulling over how much to say. "For some reason, that idiot Chief Taggart thinks I'm involved. I need to clear my name soon, before things get totally out of control."

"Do you think you should have Garrett come down sooner?" Paige asked.

I sighed. "No. He's busy in Granville. I just got off the phone with him. He's just as confused as we are as to why Taggart thinks I'm involved. He said to call him after I get back from the police station tomorrow morning."

"So what are you and Aunt Shirley planning?"

"I don't exactly know yet. I think tomorrow morning you, Aunt Shirley, and I should go to the station. Afterward we will stop by the bakery and see how your cake is coming. And maybe..." I trailed off knowing she was going to have a fit.

"What? Just say it."

I leaned up on my elbow. "I think we should stop by Julie's house to see if we can find out something."

"We can't go inside her house. I'm sure it's covered in police tape."

"I didn't exactly say we'd go inside," I said. "I'm thinking maybe look through the windows, something like that. I'll pull her address up on my navigation app in the morning."

Paige plopped down on her back. "I don't want to go to jail a day before my wedding, Ryli."

"You won't. I promise. Look, we got one cop that's such a zealot he can't see the truth, and two more that are barely out of diapers. No way are they going to be able to solve this on their own."

Paige chuckled. "You're beginning to sound more and more like Aunt Shirley every day."

I threw my pillow at her. "Don't ever say that again!"

* * *

"Are you sure you don't want me to come with you?" Mom asked the next morning at breakfast. "I have no problem going and telling that Taggart man just what I think of him."

I laughed at Mom's brevity. I bent down and kissed her head. "Thanks, but Aunt Shirley, Paige, and I can handle it. You stay here with the others and make sure the last of the food and wedding prep is done."

"I just got off the phone with Matt," Paige announced as she bounced into the kitchen. "He and Nick are leaving around eleven this morning. Hopefully they'll be here by three at the latest."

"It's nice seeing you excited again," Mom said.

"I'll be honest," Paige said as she poured milk into her cereal bowl then sat down at the table. "I've struggled a lot with being excited and happy for the wedding, and feeling sad for the deaths of Jim and Julie. It's like I don't know how I'm supposed to act."

"It's understandable," Stella said. "But just remember, you've been dreaming of this moment pretty much your whole life. You are entitled to feel happy. Don't think for one second you have to justify your feelings to us. Be happy, be excited, be in love."

"Have you finished writing your vows?" I asked Paige.

Paige groaned. "Not yet. I have an idea of what I want to say, just nothing concrete yet."

"Are we about ready?" Aunt Shirley said as she breezed into the kitchen.

Megan started giggling. I looked over at Aunt Shirley and nearly fell out of my chair.

151

"Why in the world do you even own a shirt like that?" I asked.

"What?" Aunt Shirley said, pulling the sweatshirt out and looking at it as though she'd never seen it before.

It was a bright pink sweatshirt that read: I wasn't planning on going for a run today...but those cops came out of nowhere! Two girls were sprinting for their lives down the street.

"I think it's totally appropriate," Aunt Shirley said.

I was speechless. The fact she would actually own a shirt like that was crazy. The fact she actually *packed* a shirt like that to take on vacation was even crazier. Combined with her pink and purple hair, there was no hiding Aunt Shirley.

"I think it's a lovely shirt," Mom said nonplussed.

My head snapped to my mom. "You're okay with her wearing that...to a *police station?*" I demanded.

Mom stared back at me with cool, assessing eyes. "I am when it's about something as ridiculous as my baby being accused of two murders."

Score one for Mom.

"Fine," I said to Aunt Shirley. "Just try not to antagonize anyone else today, okay?"

Aunt Shirley grinned at me. "Who...me?"

"Yes, you," I said sternly.

"No promises."

I sighed and looked at Paige. "You about ready?"

"Yep."

"Let me get my coat," Aunt Shirley said. "About time I was pulling it out."

A few minutes later the three of us piled into the Falcon and headed for the police station. My stomach was in knots by the time I found a place to park and we all went inside.

"Aunt Shirley, isn't that coat a little excessive?" I asked. "I mean, it's not like we're in the tundra right now."

Aunt Shirley pushed back the hood on her body-length, down-filled camouflage parka. I'd never seen anything so hideous—well, except for the see-through shirt she had on last night.

"This baby is good for covert operations. I draw this hood around me, and no one knows who I am. I figure it might come in handy today. We need to do some serious investigating."

On one hand, she was right. With the hood up, you couldn't see any part of her. On the other hand, no one in the world owned that coat in camouflage, so everyone would know who she was. I didn't have the heart to tell her.

Stepping into the police station, I quickly took in the surroundings. There were a couple chairs around the perimeter of the room. To the right was a door that could only be opened by punching in a code. I assumed it led to the back where the police officers were, and directly in front of us was a large glass panel with a heavy-set woman behind it. Her overly bleach-blonde hair was teased to the ceiling.

"Can I help you?" she whined.

Aunt Shirley pushed her way to the front. "We're here to see Taggart."

The woman's eyes narrowed at Aunt Shirley's tone. "*Chief* Taggart is busy right now. Take a seat, and I'll let him know you're here."

I highly doubt that.

The three of us moved to the empty chairs in the room. Paige picked up a magazine and began flipping through it. I got out my cell phone to text Garrett.

"At the police station now. Taggart is making us wait."

Less than a minute later I got a reply from Garrett. "Sounds like something he'd do. Text me when finished."

Twenty minutes later we were still in the holding area waiting on Taggart. I looked at Aunt Shirley and rolled my eyes. She smiled sweetly at me then motioned her head for me to follow her. We both stood up and walked to the window.

"How much longer is it going to be?" Aunt Shirley all but shouted.

The processed blonde looked up from her solitaire game on the computer. "I have no idea," she snapped. "Our Chief is very busy."

"Well," Aunt Shirley shouted, "you tell your Chief we came down here like he asked at the time he said. If he can't be bothered to talk with us, we'll come back at a later time. You see, we're very busy, too."

I gave the nasty blonde my best steely-eyed look. "Very busy."

"C'mon, girls," Aunt Shirley said. "Get your stuff...we're outta here."

Immediately the locked door leading to the back area was thrown open. Chief Taggart stood there scowling at us.

"Well, well," Aunt Shirley said, "looks like you got unbusy real quick."

Chief Taggart snarled at Aunt Shirley. "All of you, in here now!"

I couldn't help but grab the bull by the horns. I made a slow progression back to the chair to retrieve my purse and coat. I slowly set the magazine back on the table, taking time to straighten the magazines. By the time I walked back over to where Aunt Shirley, Paige, and Taggart were standing, I thought his head was going to explode. His face was red and his nostrils were flaring.

I ignored his obvious anger. "I believe we're all ready now, Chief. Thank you for seeing us so quickly."

Aunt Shirley and Paige snickered.

Chief Taggart put his finger in my face. "Don't tempt me, girlie. I'll haul you off to jail faster than you can imagine."

I barely refrained from rolling my eyes. I'd been threatened a lot worse than that by Garrett.

"You'll do kindly to remove your finger from my niece's face," Aunt Shirley said. "We are here out of the goodness of our hearts. You keep threatening us, and we'll have a lawyer down here so fast screaming police brutality you won't know which end is up. Don't think for one second I don't know you bullied your way into our house last night."

Taggart hitched up his pants and turned on his heel without another word. We all looked at each other and followed him silently. Officer Clark and Officer Dillon were both sitting at their desks in the middle of the room. I gave them a little wave. They both waved back then quickly looked away.

"In here," Taggart snapped and opened a door to the right. It was a tiny interrogation room, just big enough to sit four people around a table.

Taggart waited until we were seated before sitting down. He narrowed his eyes at Aunt Shirley's sweatshirt but didn't say anything.

"Since none of you are under arrest at this time, there's no need to separate you," Chief Taggart said.

At this time?

"And really, it's just you I'm interested in, Ms. Sinclair. You're the one that keeps popping up unexpectedly in my investigation."

Wonderful.

"Did you have an opportunity to question Larry Blackwell, Chief?" I asked.

Taggart's face was like granite. "I'll do the asking of the questions. You, young lady, will do the answering. Do you understand how this will work?"

I swallowed hard. "Yes. I was just curious—"

"So, how well did you know Jim Cleary?"

I took a deep breath. Obviously I'd be getting nowhere with Taggart. "I've known Jim for years. Ever since he built his house next to ours."

"And Julie Crider? How well did you know her?"

"Again, I've known Julie since childhood. When we'd stay here during the summers with my grandparents, Paige, Julie, Susie, Whitney, Debbie, and a couple other girls would always run around together."

Taggart looked down at his notebook. "That would be Susie Shoeman, Debbie Lancaster, and Whitney Lark, correct?"

"Yes." I was beginning to get annoyed.

156

"Let me just get right to it," Chief Taggart said. "Were you in love with Jim Cleary?"

The three of us laughed at that question.

"Uh…no!" I said.

Taggart narrowed his eyes at me. "Your Chief Kimble has assured me that I have the wrong girl, but I don't think so. See, you claimed to have eavesdropped on a conversation outside Jim's window the night he was murdered. You imply it was a woman, but you don't know who the woman was and you didn't see her leave."

"That's correct," I said tersely.

"I think it was *you* he was fighting with, and it was *you* that picked up the drill in anger and ran the auger through his heart."

I could feel my palms start to sweat and my pulse race.

Aunt Shirley snorted. "Then you'd be an even bigger idiot than I originally thought."

I bit my tongue to keep from laughing. Nervous laughter…it was my kryptonite.

Taggart squinted at Aunt Shirley. "I'm not asking you. I'm asking your niece. Unless you helped her murder Jim."

Aunt Shirley laughed. "Please, if I killed a man, I wouldn't leave the body out in the open where it would be discovered."

I groaned. Leave it to Aunt Shirley to get us arrested for something we didn't do!

"Hypothetically speaking, of course," Aunt Shirley added quickly.

Taggart grunted. "See, I think you were so jealous of Jim and Julie's new relationship that you drilled Jim through the heart, and you stabbed Julie with a knife through the heart. Notice how I keep coming back to the heart. This was definitely a crime of passion."

Paige started crying. "Is that how Julie died? Someone stabbed her through the heart?"

"Stabbed her once through the stomach, and then again through the heart."

My mind whirled with this information. "Why me? Why would you pick me as the killer? I haven't been here since summer. I had no idea Jim and Julie were even dating. In fact, I'm dating Chief Kimble. I'm sure he told you that. Why aren't you looking at someone who *did* know they were dating? Maybe a guy or girl that Jim was building a house for? Or maybe someone Julie was selling a house to. Someone in the—"

I cut myself off and looked quickly at Aunt Shirley. I was going to say someone in the real estate business. Someone who was jealous of Jim and Julie…someone who dealt with them both…and that person was Whitney Lark!

Could Whitney have done something like this?

"I think we've answered all your questions. Now, if you aren't going to arrest us, we'd like to leave," Aunt Shirley said.

Chief Taggart slowly looked at each of us. "I'm not arresting you right now because I know you're staying in town for a couple more days. Just know, I plan on making an arrest soon."

My heart dropped to my stomach. I could think of a handful of people the Chief should be looking at. Why was he so adamant on pinning these murders on me? Was he seriously that lazy in his duties?

The three of us got up to go. No surprise, I was moving much faster now. I just wanted out of the station as fast as possible.

The sunshine hitting the white snow hurt my eyes as we walked out of the police station. It must have been a lot darker inside the station than I realized. Squinting against the sun—wishing I'd brought sunglasses—I got behind the wheel of the Falcon. I laid my head against the steering wheel.

"Don't worry, Ryli. Matt will be here in a few hours," Paige said, "and Garrett will be here tomorrow. They will figure out what to do."

I lifted my head off the steering wheel. "This is my mess, Paige. I appreciate you trying to encourage me, but this is my fight. I want to solve this case on my own, not run to Garrett and Matt because someone is being mean to me."

Aunt Shirley slapped me on the shoulder. "Atta girl! This isn't anything we can't solve. Granted, there's a whole town full of people that may have wanted those two dead, but I'm thinking it's someone close to them. You know what they say…most victims know their killers. And Taggart was right about one thing, it may have been a crime of passion."

"Right," I said, starting the car and heading toward Susie's bakery. "I think it's time to push Susie a little harder. I want to know what Taggart asked her."

CHAPTER 20

There were only three customers in the bakery when we entered. Susie was getting orders around while another girl behind the counter was ringing them up. I figured the girl was Carrie, the one Josh had a crush on.

The customers got their orders and headed out the door.

"Hi, guys. Can I get you something?" Susie asked.

"How about some coffee for us?" I suggested. "Then do you think you could sit with us for a second?"

"Of course."

A few minutes later Susie came over to a table carrying four cups of coffee in a travel tray. She set the tray down and slid into the empty chair.

"This is the first time I've sat down all morning," she said. "I went to the station around six o'clock so I wouldn't be late opening up. Carrie finished getting the last of the donuts and scones out while I was gone."

I looked over at the girl wiping down the counter. She had earbuds in and was humming along to the music coming through her earbuds.

"We just came back, too," Aunt Shirley informed Susie. "How long were you there?"

"Not long. Chief Taggart basically asked me what time I arrived at the party. What was I doing around four o'clock that afternoon?" Susie looked at me sheepishly. "He wanted to know if

I saw you at any time that afternoon between three and five…maybe hanging around Julie's place."

"Are you serious?" I said disgustedly. "I have no idea why this creep has it out for me, but this is ridiculous!"

"Don't worry," Susie said hurriedly. "I told him I hadn't seen you at all until I arrived at the party." She dropped her chin to her chest and sighed. "The truth is, I closed up shop a little early. I was looking for Jolene most of the afternoon."

"Jolene?" Paige asked.

Susie closed her eyes for a moment. Then reached for her coffee. "I haven't seen Jolene since Friday morning. She came to the bakery to see if she could borrow my car. I told her no. We had a fight. I tried calling her cell a bunch of times, but she didn't answer. So I closed up the shop and left."

"Did you find her?" Paige asked.

"No. I went out to her trailer, looked around there, but nothing. I found all sorts of things I didn't want to see, but I didn't find her. So I came back to the shop, picked up the cupcakes I'd already prepared for your party, then went home to shower and get ready."

"So are you saying you haven't heard from your sister in over twenty-four hours?" I asked.

Susie nodded. "That's right. But this isn't the first time she's pulled a disappearing act. She did this a few weeks back, too." Susie swiped at a tear that escaped. "That's when I first realized she was using again. I went out to her trailer and saw the drugs."

"Did you tell Chief Taggart she's missing?" Paige asked.

Susie bit her lip. "No. The thing is, I don't think the Chief would take it seriously. He doesn't exactly…he doesn't…"

"He doesn't think a lot of your sister and her lifestyle?" Aunt Shirley asked.

Susie met her eyes. "No, he doesn't."

"Maybe we could drive by her mobile home since you're busy here today," Paige said. "You know, see if she's there but not taking your calls."

Susie grabbed Paige's hand. "Thank you. I'd appreciate it. Now, I better get back to work. I have a wedding cake to put the finishing touches on."

Once Susie gave us Jolene's address, we finished the coffee and decided to head out. We still had to drive by Julie's place and see what we could find out there.

I was heading out the door when Susie called me over to the display case. I gave Paige the keys to unlock the car and told them I'd be right there.

"Ryli, I wanted to tell you something without Paige around. I wanted it to be a surprise. I have one of those wedding archways in my garage. I was wondering if you'd want to use it—I mean, if you aren't already using the flower shop's archway."

"I love that idea!" I said. "We actually didn't rent one from the flower shop."

Susie bit her lip. "The thing is, it's pretty large and bulky. Carrie has church Sunday morning, and you know I can't rely on Jolene. I totally hate to ask this, but do you think you'd have time to run by my house and help me load it on Sunday?"

"It's no problem at all. I have to run into town anyway around eleven to pick up the flowers, so I can probably swing by around eleven-fifteen if that's okay?"

Susie clapped her hands together. "That's perfect! After seeing the layout of your house Friday night, I realized the archway would be a beautiful touch. And with everything that's gone on the last few days, I really wanted to give Paige something extra special. Let me give you my address."

I got her address and gave her a hug. "That's so thoughtful of you, Susie. It's been very hard for Paige to get excited about the wedding with all that's gone on."

"You girls be careful today. And I'll see you around eleven-fifteen tomorrow. Call me if you find out anything about Jolene, please."

"Will do."

I jogged over to the Falcon and got in.

"What was that about?" Paige asked.

"Last-minute wedding stuff."

I wasn't exactly sure where Julie lived. I searched her name on the Internet and was able to get a current street name. I didn't figure the house would be too hard to find, what with the crime scene tape up and all.

A few minutes later and we were creeping along Pike Street at a snail's pace. The houses on this side of town were not located within water's distance. I guess growing up here and having access to the lake all the time made Julie not want to live directly on it.

"There it is," Paige said, pointing to a cute, one-story house. Well, cute if you didn't take into account the fact it had police tape all over the front door. There was a one-car garage and the house was no bigger than twelve hundred square feet. Large picture windows surrounded each side of the front door.

"How are we going to look through the windows without everyone seeing?" I asked.

"We're going in through the back. Pull down the side street here and park," Aunt Shirley commanded.

"Maybe we should do this tonight," Paige suggested.

I looked in my rear-view mirror at her. "Tonight? When Matt and Nick are here? How do you suggest the three of us go about that without attracting unwanted attention?"

Paige stuck her tongue out at me. "It was just a suggestion."

"If we're lucky, she either didn't lock her dead bolt to the back of the house, or she doesn't have one. If it's just a standard lock, I can get us in," Aunt Shirley said.

"No! No way are we breaking into Julie's house!" Paige said, sitting up straight in her seat. "I didn't realize we would be breaking and entering. I just thought we were looking through windows!"

I looked over at Aunt Shirley. I hated to pull Paige into this, but there's no way I wasn't going inside that house. I needed to see for myself what the crime scene looked like.

"You aren't going in," Aunt Shirley said calmly to Paige. "You're gonna be the look out. Your job is to sit in the car and make sure no one comes. If they do, text Ryli and let her know. Ryli, put your phone on vibrate."

I did what Aunt Shirley requested. "Now, who has a plastic card we can use? It may or may not get damaged. I can't guarantee anything."

164

I rummaged around in my wallet. "I have an old library card, will that work?"

Aunt Shirley held out her hand. "It'll do."

Paige scooted over to the window closest to the street so she could see clearly. Aunt Shirley and I casually made our way through the back of Julie's yard. Luckily the snow muffled any sound we might have made.

We scurried up the two stairs and onto a sparsely decorated wooden deck. A small table with two chairs took up one side of the deck, and a large gas grill took up the other side.

Aunt Shirley bent down and stuck the library card down by the door handle. She gave it a few slides. I was still a little skeptical it would work. I'd just looked over my shoulder to make sure no one was coming down the street when I heard the click.

Aunt Shirley gave me a saucy grin. "I'm in."

The back door opened into a tiny laundry room off the kitchen. A small welcome rug greeted us.

"Make sure you wipe your feet off on that rug," I said. "I don't want us traipsing snow throughout the house."

"This ain't my first rodeo, kid. I know what I'm doing."

I rolled my eyes and walked into the miniscule kitchen. "So what exactly are we looking for?" There were dishes piled in the sink, with lots of caked on yuckiness. "Obviously she was too distraught over Jim to do dishes."

"I'm not exactly sure what we're looking for. Something that doesn't fit," Aunt Shirley said.

We tiptoed into the living room, careful to stay away from the windows. I gasped when I got my first good look at the room. There were bloodstains on the couch and on the carpet.

"I just wasn't expecting it," I said.

"I know. It's always hard. I'd say she was stabbed over here while they were both standing. Notice how there are tiny splatters that lead to the couch. So then Julie stumbles over to the couch…probably surprised and hurting."

I let out a little sob. I couldn't help myself. I hated the thought of Julie being in pain like that. She was such a nice person.

Aunt Shirley gave me a sympathetic look before she continued. "Then I'd say she just sat down on the couch to die. Taggart said she was stabbed in the stomach and the heart, but I can't tell if she was stabbed in the stomach while standing and then immediately in the heart, or if she was stabbed in the heart while she was sitting on the couch. I'm not an expert in blood splatter."

I held up my hand. "Enough. Let's just see what we can find."

I looked around the living room and saw countless wadded up tissues on the end table. I guess whoever processed the scene didn't think they needed to collect all the tissues.

"She'd obviously been crying over Jim, which makes sense," I said.

I ran my hands around the cushions.

"Anything?" Aunt Shirley asked. She unzipped her camo parka and lifted her sweatshirt over her hands to make sure she didn't leave fingerprints while she rummaged through the end table drawer.

"Nothing," I said. I knelt down to feel around under the couch. I heard a noise and looked up. Aunt Shirley was heading down a hallway.

"Where are you going?" I hissed. "We need to stay together in case Paige texts."

"Don't get your panties in a bunch. I gotta pee."

"Are you crazy! You can't use the bathroom at a murder scene. It's trashy."

Aunt Shirley peeked her head back around the corner to me. "When you get to be my age, you'll understand. When you gotta go, you gotta go. My bladder dictates my life."

Shaking my head, I started feeling under the couch again. Figuring if I had some light it would go faster, I got out my cell phone and pulled up the flashlight app. Wiggling the light under the couch, I saw something near one of the couch legs. I made a grab for it when my phone vibrated in my hand. Without looking at what I found, I slipped it in my pocket. I quickly shut off the flashlight app and opened my text.

It was from Paige. "Cops! Get out now!"

"Aunt Shirley, we need to go...now!"

Silence.

I glanced out the large picture window and saw Officer Dillon pulling into the driveway. Officer Clark was with him. "Aunt Shirley!"

"I hear ya! Go, go! I'll go out this way."

I pivoted, crouched low, and ran through the living room. It wasn't until I'd skidded through the kitchen and into the laundry room that I realized there was probably no door for Aunt Shirley to escape out of. Heart thumping wildly in my chest, I was about to turn around and go fetch her when I heard the front door open.

Grabbing the back door with my sweater, I silently opened it and locked the bottom lock. I could hear the two officers talking in

167

the living room. I slipped out the back door and eased the door shut behind me.

Praying none of the boards creaked, I made my way across the deck and down the two stairs. Once my feet hit the snow, I took off like a rocket toward the Falcon. I could see Paige jumping up and down inside the car, motioning for me to hurry.

I glanced over my right shoulder and about had a heart attack. A window screen flew off the window and landed in the snow. Slowing my pace, I watched in horror as Aunt Shirley threw a leg over the ledge of the windowsill. Next came an arm. Unfortunately, she couldn't right herself enough to throw the other leg over. She fell sideways out the window.

Thud!

She landed so hard snow flew in all directions. I hoped her huge parka cushioned some of the fall. Before I could change directions and run to help her, she looked up and saw me. Motioning for me to keep going, I sprinted toward the Falcon…the whole time watching her.

I knew she had to be crawling on her hands and knees, but the parka was so huge, all I could see was this large lump of camouflage moving swiftly in the snow over to the back side of the house. Using the corner of the house, she slowly eased her way up to a standing position. Looking in both directions to make sure the coast was clear, she took off across the lawn toward the Falcon.

I reached down and pulled the car door open and slid inside. I could hear Paige screaming in the backseat, but my brain couldn't process what she was saying. I hadn't had an adrenaline rush like this since I was plied with ketamine and chased through the church with a knife.

168

"Oh, man that was fun! Go, go, go," Aunt Shirley cried as she slid into the passenger's seat. On automatic, my hands went up and started the car. I fishtailed out onto the street and started driving. I had no idea where I was going.

I got to the end of the road and pulled over again. "What're you doing?" Aunt Shirley demanded.

I looked down at my hands on the steering wheel…they were shaking. "I just need a minute."

"Are you okay?" Paige whispered. "You look pale and your hands are shaking."

I took a deep breath. "I haven't felt this panicked in a while. Not since…"

"Understandable," Aunt Shirley said without much sympathy. "But remember we have a job to do, and that's to keep your butt out of jail." She let out a little yell. "Man, I miss these days!"

Knowing she was right, and I didn't want to spend even an hour in jail, much less the rest of my life, I gave myself a little shake. "I found something," I said and dug in my coat pocket to retrieve the item that was under the sofa.

Paige leaned up from the back seat and Aunt Shirley turned to me. I opened my palm and revealed a syringe.

"Oh boy," Paige whispered. "Now what do we do?"

I looked at Aunt Shirley. "Only two people I know that use syringes…Whitney and Jolene."

CHAPTER 21

"Where did Whitney say she was going to be today?" Aunt Shirley asked.

"Just give me a minute to think," I said. "I'd been drinking a lot last night, so my mind is a little fuzzy."

Aunt Shirley closed her eyes. "She said two houses. She was showing two houses, one was on Murray Street or something like that."

Paige hit the seat in front of her, startling Aunt Shirley. "I remember! It was Montgomery. She was showing a house on Montgomery and a house on Sage. I remember Sage because I remember giggling in my head and wondering if the house on Sage would smell like sage."

I laughed. "Good one. So which house? I'm thinking Sage because it's so late in the morning, she's probably already shown Montgomery."

"Agreed," Aunt Shirley said. "I just hope that's the order she went in."

Paige pulled up Google Maps on her phone and typed in Sage Street. A few seconds later, I was heading toward the outskirts of town. I pulled onto a paved road. The houses out here were spread out a little farther since it was lakefront property. Each house had a private dock that led to the water.

I was beginning to think we'd made a mistake when I heard Aunt Shirley yell. "There! The house on the right, and it looks like cars are there."

I saw where she was pointing. It was an impressive house, no doubt. It was also recently built. There was still a sign stating it was a Jim Cleary house in the front yard next to the For Sale sign.

I didn't pull into the small drive. Instead I simply pulled over as far as I could and let the Falcon idle. No one said a word, we just watched as the front door opened and Whitney came down the stairs followed by a young couple holding hands.

I turned off the car. "How do you wanna play this?"

"Straight up," Aunt Shirley said. "I say we tell her what we found and see how she reacts."

We watched as Whitney shook their hands and handed them a business card. The young couple got in their car, backed out, then took off in the opposite direction.

I pushed open my door. "Let's go."

Whitney was still standing in the front yard doing a small victory dance.

"I guess that means it went well," I said, making Whitney scream. It was exactly what I'd wanted to do.

"Don't scare me like that!" Whitney patted herself on the chest and scowled at me. "You gave me a fright. What are you doing here?"

"We came to ask you a few questions," I said.

"What kind of questions?" Whitney hedged.

"We found one of your syringes at Julie's house," Aunt Shirley said. "Care to explain?"

Whitney frowned. "Why were you at Julie's house? It should be off limits. I drove by it this morning and there was still police tape up."

"Care to explain the syringe?" Aunt Shirley asked again.

Whitney's eyes narrowed and she crossed her arms in front of her chest. "I don't have to tell you anything. And the fact you went into Julie's house when it still has police tape around it is against the law. It's called breaking and entering in case you didn't know."

I pulled the syringe out of my coat pocket. "Here's the syringe we found. Like Aunt Shirley said, care to explain?"

Whitney's mouth dropped open. "Omigod, did you pick it up? Your fingerprints are all over it now. You contaminated a crime scene! My uncle is gonna be so mad!"

Did she say uncle?

"Who's your uncle?" I asked.

Whitney looked down her nose at us. "Chief Taggart."

"Does he have family all over this town?" I muttered.

"How do you think I knew Julie's whereabouts and when Jim would come into her office to see her?" Whitney sneered. "Tammi and I are cousins. Her mom and my mom are Chief Taggart's little sisters."

Breathing at this point was almost becoming painful. I was honestly terrified.

"And let me tell you, he's gonna be livid you went into Julie's house and took something!" Whitney let out a harsh laugh. "I bet he doesn't waste any time hauling you in. He told me this morning after your little visit to the station that he was going to let you stew a little, get you all worked up over the fact he was going to arrest you in a few days." Whitney's eyes took on a wild look. "But after this little stunt, I bet he arrests you by tonight!"

"Now wait just a minute," Aunt Shirley said. I was glad she could talk because my mouth was so dry I couldn't even open it. I could feel myself shaking. "No one said we were inside the house. We also drove by and saw the police tape. We decided to look in the windows and see if we could see something relevant to the case. We found the syringe on the back deck in plain view."

I needed to practice my lying. Aunt Shirley did it so well *I* actually believed what she was saying. "So don't go gettin' your panties in a bunch. No need to call your uncle." Aunt Shirley paused as if thinking. "Oh, and we also noticed a screen was pushed out, too. I don't know if that means anything."

Paige let out a nervous giggle.

Whitney whipped her head around to glare at Paige. "I almost wish I'd have stuck around last night just to see my uncle make you sweat."

I jerked back as if she'd slapped me. Truth was, I wouldn't have been more surprised if she had. "Wait, I just realized something. Last night when you were texting on your phone before you suddenly left...were you talking with your uncle? Did he tell you Julie had been murdered and he was coming out to question us?"

Whitney shrugged. "Again, I don't have to tell you anything. Although I will say, I don't know how a syringe got on Julie's deck. Maybe Julie was using drugs. I mean, I doubt it, she was too fat to be a drug user." Whitney suddenly laughed. "Maybe Jo the Ho was supplying Julie with drugs."

What is it with this family and name calling?

"All I know," Whitney continued, "is you better stay away from me, or I seriously will call my uncle and tell him what you did. Trust me, he's dying to haul you in for these murders." Whitney turned and sashayed toward her car. She yanked the door open and glared at us. "One more thing, that's not mine. The needle size is wrong." Whitney yanked the car door closed and sped away.

We all stood in silence...too stunned to speak.

"Well, at least we know why Taggart seems more and more inclined to pin these murders on you," Aunt Shirley said.

"And why's that?" I asked.

"Could be he's trying to take the heat off his niece," Aunt Shirley said.

"What do you think she meant by the needle size?" Paige asked as we headed for the Falcon.

"Not sure," I said. "I guess we need to do some research on that. Let's stop by the trailer park real quick to see about Jolene before we head home."

It wasn't too hard to find the trailer park where Jolene lived. There were only about fifteen other trailers in the park, each one looking sadder and sadder than the last. It was hard to believe that something so ugly and trashy could be mixed in with the hundred thousand dollar and million dollar homes the lake boasted. The trailers were eerily quiet considering it was the day before New Year's Eve. I figured most of the residents didn't get around too early in the morning...they were probably more night owls.

Paige read off the trailer number from the address Susie had given us. It didn't take long to locate the dilapidated, singlewide heap sitting in front of us.

"Well, isn't this a nice pile of dung," Aunt Shirley said as stepped out of the Falcon.

At one time I'd say the trailer had been white, but now there was a plethora of browns and grays covering the outer aluminum panels. There was a fist-size hole in the door that had been patched with duct tape. It wasn't even the cute, colorful duct tape you can buy nowadays. Nope, this was just the traditional silver quick fix stuff.

Plop! Plop!

I looked down at my phone and saw it was a text from Debbie.

"Debbie wants to know if we can stop by real quick," I said. "Guess she's having a hard time today."

"Sure," Paige said.

I texted her we'd be over shortly. She sent back her address. I slipped the phone back in my pocket and looked up at the nasty, run-down trailer.

None of us were eager to walk up the broken wooden steps that led to Jolene's front door.

"Careful where you walk and what you touch," I advised. "We don't have time to get a Tetanus shot today."

"Well, let's get this over with," Aunt Shirley mumbled as she carefully started up the broken steps.

I wasn't sure the tiny deck would hold all our weight. The ominous creak from the stairs every time Aunt Shirley moved made the spit in my mouth dry up.

Think thin…think thin! I chanted over and over in my head as I slowly made my way up the stairs. I glanced back to make sure Paige was close on my heels. I didn't want to leave her outside for fear of something happening to her. The area didn't exactly scream safe, friendly neighborhood.

"Jolene," Aunt Shirley said, knocking on the splintered and patched door. "Are you in there?"

Silence.

Aunt Shirley gripped the handle and twisted. None of us were really shocked when the door swung open. I couldn't imagine there was much inside that needed locked and protected.

The smell of rotten eggs, sewer, and cat urine permeating throughout the little trailer had my stomach rolling. I put my hand up over my mouth and nose to try and block the smell. Paige did the same thing.

Directly in front of us was the living room. It was sparsely decorated with one broken-down and dangerously sagging brown couch facing a TV that had to be thirty years old. There were no pictures or decorations on the walls, and there was no other furniture to really speak of. To our left was a tiny kitchen that didn't even have a kitchen table. I'm sure there were countertops, but you couldn't see them because of all the trash and old food covering them.

The hallway to our right was so narrow a heavier person would have to turn sideways just to walk down it. Craning my neck, I could see three doors down the constricted passageway. I didn't even want to venture what the bedrooms and bathroom looked like.

My stomach rolled and pitched again. We needed to get out fast before I lost what little I had in my stomach.

The piles and piles of trash littering the floor was mindboggling. I'd never seen anything so filthy in my life. Fast food wrapper, putrid milk jugs, animal feces…you name it, it was on the floor.

"I'm thinking someone should have given her a garbage can as a housewarming gift," Paige said matter-of-factly.

I snorted repeatedly through my hand. Well, it was more a laugh, but with my hand covering up my vital breathing parts, it came out like little snorts.

"Maybe a mop and broom," Paige continued.

I smacked her on the arm. "Stop, you're making me laugh, and I don't want to take in any more air than I already have to!"

"Look over there," Aunt Shirley said, pointing to a metal TV tray sitting next to the sagging couch.

I took a step forward to see what she was pointing to, kicking trash out of my way. It didn't take long for my eyes to hone in on the syringe. I knew I needed to look at the needle size like Whitney had made reference to, but I didn't want to risk walking across the room. God only knew what might grab me.

"Hey," a deep male voice said behind us, "where's Jolene?"

Whirling around, my eyes widened at the sudden appearance of the scruffy-looking guy. I couldn't tell his age, but I placed him between twenty to twenty-five years old. He had on greasy gray sweats and a matching dirty sweatshirt.

Usually I'd be a little more afraid being alone with a young male in a seedy place. However, his sunken cheekbones and emaciated body told me that even *we* could take him if we had to.

"I said where's Jo?" The man scratched his head, his wild eyes darting around the trailer.

"We haven't seen her in a few days," Aunt Shirley said. "When's the last time you saw her?"

Scrawny shrugged his bony shoulders. "What day is it today?"

I rolled my eyes. "What do you want with her?" Not that I really cared to hear the answer.

He laughed. "I got me an itch that Jo usually scratches." He literally reached down and scratched himself. "You get my drift?"

I barely refrained from gagging and throwing up in my mouth. "Well, as you can see, she isn't here." I hoped he'd take the hint and leave.

He didn't. Instead, his glazed-over eyes looked us up and down slowly. I was definitely going to shower when I got home. "Since she's not here," Scrawny shrugged, "how's about one of you? I got ten bucks."

Aunt Shirley guffawed. "Ten bucks? Ha! You ain't seeing my goodies for no ten bucks!"

Scrawny wrinkled his nose. "I wasn't exactly thinking of you, grandma. I was thinking of one of you broads." He pointed between Paige and me.

"First off," Aunt Shirley said, "you'd be lucky to have a go at someone like me. I'd rock your world, little boy."

"Eewww!" I exclaimed. "Gross!"

Scrawny shrugged again. "I guess maybe I could give you a go. You do have cool hair."

"Aunt Shirley," Paige hissed, "just stop talking. You're going to get us in trouble."

178

Scrawny lunged toward Paige. I leaped onto his back and started beating him over the head with my hands, screaming obscenities at him the whole time. Turning in circles he tried to shove me off.

"Stand back," Aunt Shirley shouted as she reached inside her coat and unzipped a pocket. I jumped off Scrawny's back and gave him a good shove. He stumbled and would've gone down but the antiquated TV caught his fall. I quickly pulled Paige toward me.

"This is for thinking we were easy, scumbag!" Aunt Shirley aimed the can of Mace and sprayed with everything she had. The guy's screams of pain had my hairs standing on end. We needed to get out of there and fast.

"Let's go!" I yelled and shoved Paige out the door with my right hand and grabbed hold of Aunt Shirley's parka with my left. I yanked Aunt Shirley through the front door just as Scrawny clamored to his feet.

"When I catch up to you," Scrawny shouted, shaking his head like a dog getting out of water, "you bitches are gonna pay!"

I already had my keys out as we stumbled down the stairs and jumped into the Falcon. My hands were shaking uncontrollably as I shoved the key into the ignition. The Falcon roared to life. I careened out of the tiny yard as Scrawny staggered out of the door, tears streaming down his red face, fist shaking in the air.

Aunt Shirley rolled down her window and flipped him the bird. "Catch that you sick piece of animal dung!" Laughing, she rolled the window back up. "God I miss being a private eye." She turned in her seat and grinned at me. "I'm thinking about coming out of retirement."

God help us all.

CHAPTER 22

Paige pulled up directions on how to get to Debbie's house. She was outside the city limits—almost to a neighboring town across the lake.

I turned off the blacktop road and onto a well-maintained gravel road. A few minutes later a modest two-story house appeared on the left. There were numerous snow-covered plastic toys in the front yard, along with a large, wooden swing set off the side of the house.

"I'd say this is it," I said. I pulled the Falcon into the driveway and shut off the car.

The front door was immediately opened and Debbie stepped out, a tow-headed baby jiggling on her hip. "C'mon in ladies. I'm so glad you could stop by." Her voice broke and she wiped away a tear.

Debbie led us through a messy living room—where two young girls were dancing along with a video on the TV—and into an even messier kitchen overlooking the lake. Debbie's house seemed to be nestled in a small channel off the main portion of the lake. It was nice and cozy.

"Sorry about the mess. With all three kids home on Christmas vacation, it's nearly impossible to keep the house clean."

"Don't worry about it," Paige said. "I'm sure in a few years I'll be saying the same thing."

My heart pitched. Paige's constant reminder that her life would soon change was still hard for me to process fully. It scared me to think my best friend was starting a new chapter in her life—and this time it didn't fully include me.

Aunt Shirley whistled and walked over to the bay window where the kitchen table sat. "That's a nice boat."

Debbie laughed. "Hazards of a husband who sells boats for a living. Mark loves his Sea Ray."

To me it looked like a large, white boat with a lot of room in the front to sit people. I'm sure to people who know boats it was a lot more than that. Mostly it reeked of money.

"How're you doing?" Paige asked.

Debbie blinked back tears. "I just don't understand this. I mean, I just spoke with Julie the other day. Everything was fine. I don't understand why someone would want to kill her."

I exchanged a silent look with Aunt Shirley. I wasn't sure how much we should tell Debbie. No sense dragging her into the mess, but maybe she'd have insight to Whitney and Jolene's relationship and we could narrow down our suspects even more.

At this point I was willing to scratch Blackwell's name off the list. I couldn't give a motive as to why he would want to kill both Jim and Julie.

"Momma, can we have some goldfish crackers?" A brown-haired girl came running into the room wearing a purple tutu. Her hair was pulled up into two pigtails and she was missing a front tooth.

"This is my oldest, Sarah. Sarah, can you say hi to everyone?"

The little girl tucked her chin down to her chest and scuffed her ballet slippers on the floor. "Hi."

Another little girl with blonde pigtails and sporting a pink tutu came barreling into the kitchen. "Goldfish, goldfish," she chanted as she effortlessly leaped into the air repeatedly.

Debbie handed the baby off to Sarah. "Take your brother with you in the other room while I talk." The little girl made a face but didn't say anything. Debbie then shoved a gigantic bag of goldfish to the smaller, dancing one. "Don't drop these all over the floor, Tia. And please don't let your brother mash them into the carpet."

Tia stopped jumping and stared at her mom. "No promises."

Aunt Shirley laughed. "I like her."

The little girl skipped over to Aunt Shirley. Something told me the kid never walked anywhere. "I like your hair."

Aunt Shirley dropped into a chair at the kitchen table. Tia leaped into Aunt Shirley's lap and began playing with Aunt Shirley's hair.

"Pretty colors," Tia said, sifting her fingers through Aunt Shirley's hair. She giggled as the bright colors now stood up in spikes around Aunt Shirley's head.

"I want some, Mommy," Tia demanded.

Debbie rolled her eyes. "I need you to go into the living room with your sister and brother. Mommy needs to talk with the grown-ups right now."

This didn't faze the girl in the least. She crossed her arms and stared her mother down. "I want pretty hair."

Debbie sighed. "Your daddy would kill me if I did that to your hair." Debbie quickly added, "No offense, Aunt Shirley."

Aunt Shirley smiled. "None taken. And you," Aunt Shirley said as she jiggled her knees and smiled as the little girl threw her arms in the air and squealed in delight, "have to be older to have awesome hair like this."

Tia stopped smiling and crossed her arms again. "Then I want to be older now."

Just when I was thinking the kid was a huge pain, Aunt Shirley declared, "I *really* like this kid. Reminds me a lot of myself."

Oh, boy!

Panic flashed in Debbie's eyes. Guess she didn't much like the sound of that declaration, either. "Tia, Mommy needs you to go into the living room now." I guess Tia knew that tone because she quickly hopped down from Aunt Shirley's lap.

"Goldfish, goldfish, goldfish," Tia chanted as she threw her hands in the air and skipped out of the kitchen and into the living room.

Debbie sighed. "That one will be the death of me." She turned toward the coffee pot. "Can I get anyone some coffee, water?"

"How about some coffee," Aunt Shirley said, setting Debbie at ease.

Debbie busied herself with the coffee. She set the pot on a flat, silicone potholder in front of us on the table. Next she set out cream and sugar. With nothing else to do, she sat down. The poor woman looked dead on her feet.

"I just keep running this through my mind," Debbie said as she stirred some cream and sugar into her coffee. "I don't know who would do this to both Julie and Jim. It makes no sense. At first

I thought maybe it was a robbery or something at Jim's place, but now I don't know what to think."

No one said anything while we fixed our coffee.

"What can you tell me about Whitney and Jolene?" Aunt Shirley asked.

Just jump right in there, Aunt Shirley.

Debbie tilted her head. "Like are they friends? Do they hang out? No, I don't believe so."

Aunt Shirley tried again. "Do they like each other?"

Debbie grunted. "Not hardly. But then again, Jolene doesn't seem to like any of us. It's like she blames us for taking Susie in, watching over her, when everything went bad years ago."

"Do you think Jolene could've killed Jim and Julie?" I asked.

You could have heard a pin drop in the kitchen. We all waited with baited breath as Debbie mulled it over. "How? I mean, she's usually so strung out on whatever drug she's doing that she can hardly function. She'd have to get the upper hand on both Jim and Julie. I just don't see that happening."

I did. Drugs could make a person have superhuman strength. I've watched those videos on Facebook and YouTube.

"What's Whitney's deal?" Aunt Shirley asked. "I get why she doesn't like Jolene. But why did she hate Julie?"

Debbie stared down at her coffee before answering. "When the fire first happened and Susie didn't have anywhere to go, all of us girls wanted to take her in. But the truth was, most of us couldn't. Even our parents wanted to, but it just wasn't feasible. Except Julie. Her parents could afford it. So that's where Susie went. It wasn't a big deal, we were just glad we got to stay together. But Whitney was so jealous. You know how she always wanted to be something she wasn't. And the fact Julie was able to take her in just ate at Whitney. She really started making Julie's life miserable." Debbie blew on her coffee then took a tentative sip. "I mean, Susie always made Whitney stop, but when Susie wasn't around, Whitney was horrible to Julie."

"So it wouldn't be a leap for Whitney to finally snap if the man she wanted went for Julie?"

Debbie's coffee cup landed with a heavy thud on the table. "Omigod! Do you think that's what's happened? Whitney killed Jim and Julie?" Tears fell from her eyes.

"Now, we aren't saying that," Aunt Shirley said. The sternness in her voice had Debbie nodding. "We're just asking questions is all."

Aunt Shirley may not be saying it, but as far as I was concerned, Whitney just moved to suspect number one in my book…incorrect needle size or not.

* * *

The rest of the ride home was silent. We were all lost in our own thoughts. I was trying to put all the pieces together, but I needed to see it on paper. I glanced in the rearview mirror and met Paige's eye.

"I'm thinking we don't mention any of this to Matt, okay?" Paige said.

I grinned at her. "Duh! He finds out what we do on the side, he'll have a coronary. That means he'll die, and I'll never have nieces and nephews to spoil."

I was happy to hear Paige chuckle. I was worried what all this was doing to her nerves. She was getting married in twenty-

186

four hours, and instead of primping and relaxing, she was being a lookout for a B&E and running from a drugged-out rapist.

Not our best day…but not our worst day, either.

Pulling into the driveway to the lake house, I couldn't help but look over at Jim's house. On those rare times when we shared a beer together, I'd really gotten to know and like him. Now I'd never have those times again.

"Hurry, hurry," Paige chanted behind me. "I see the guys are here. I really need to see Matt right now."

Coming to a stop in front of the house, Paige flung open the car door and jumped out. Matt must have been watching for us, because he'd already bounded down the stairs before Paige even closed the car door.

I tried to tune out their mushy hello. Mainly because I was jealous. I really missed Garrett. I'd started to become more and more dependent upon him over the months. Watching Matt and Paige together just left me lonely.

Aunt Shirley patted me on the arm. "C'mon, let's go inside and get a drink. I can't take much more of these two lovebirds necking."

Following my nose I walked into the kitchen—only to see my mom canoodling with Doc Powell. Doc was our local veterinarian. When all the stuff went down with the murders a few months back, I honestly thought Doc might be involved. But it seems the "big secret" he was keeping wasn't he was a murderer…it was he was seeing my mom.

"Doc," I cried, giving him a long hug. "I'm glad you're here."

Doc hugged me back. "I wouldn't miss it. I was able to get away from the clinic and decided to ride down with Matt and Nick.

I snagged a stuffed mushroom and shoved it in my mouth.

"Hey, not too many," Mom scolded. "Those are for after the rehearsal tonight."

"Just making sure they're good enough to serve," I laughed.

I'd almost forgotten about the wedding rehearsal. The preacher at the church we occasionally attend while staying at the lake house agreed to marry Paige and Matt. Since Nick and I were the only ones standing up with Matt and Paige, I didn't figure the rehearsal would take too long.

Mom narrowed her cool eyes at me. "Did everything go okay in town?"

I quickly popped one more mushroom in my mouth, keeping me from saying something I shouldn't. She's good at catching me in lies. Realizing I couldn't stall forever, I slowly swallowed the mushroom. "Everything went fine. Chief Taggart mainly asked for our alibis. Also, why we thought someone would want to murder both Jim and Julie."

I could tell by her skepticism she didn't exactly believe me. "Did he say who he thought committed the murders?" Mom asked, still staring me down.

I was glad I wasn't sitting down or I'd be squirming in my chair. "Well," I hedged, "he said he had someone in mind…and that an arrest would be coming soon."

I grabbed one more mushroom and shove it in my mouth, grinning at her.

"I'm sorry to hear about your friends," Doc said.

I swallowed the mushroom past the sudden lump in my throat. "Thanks. It's been a rough week, that's for sure."

"Go get freshened up," Mom said. "The preacher should be here in a couple hours. Afterward we'll have some finger foods."

Jogging down the stairs to my bedroom, I pulled out my phone and called Garrett. It went straight to voicemail. I left a message telling him to call me whenever he got the chance. I wanted to tell him about my interview at the police station.

Grabbing clean clothes to change into for the rehearsal, I headed for the shower. I desperately wanted to wash the stench of the day off my body.

CHAPTER 23

Thirty minutes later I was feeling like a new woman. Changing into a long-sleeve gray and black maxi dress, I left my hair to dry naturally. A quick swipe of mascara and lipstick and I was ready for the rehearsal.

"How'd it go?" Megan asked as I walked out of the downstairs bathroom.

"Fine. I think the Chief still thinks I'm involved. I don't want Mom to worry though."

"I could tell she was a little worried this morning, but she totally tried not to let on." Megan shifted her clothes in her hands. "Well, I'm going to jump in the shower if you're done. We finished everything upstairs for tonight and tomorrow."

I knew how hard they'd all been working to make this so perfect for Paige. On impulse I reached out and hugged her. "Thanks for everything you've done for Paige."

Megan smiled. "She's my cousin, and I love her. I'd do anything for her. I just wish things could've gone a little better for her this week."

"Me, too."

"Okay, out of my way…I wanna look extra good tonight. That Nick is a cutie." She winked at me and walked into the bathroom.

I laughed and couldn't have agreed more. Nick was a cutie.

I opened my bedroom door and nearly gagged. "Get a room, you two!" Paige and Matt were snuggled up on her twin bed acting like they hadn't seen each other in years instead of a few days.

"Go away, Ryli," Matt said between kisses.

"Mom catches you down here and she'll skin you alive," I taunted. They both threw pillows at me...never once coming up for air.

Deciding to bow out gracefully, I headed upstairs to bounce around a few theories with Aunt Shirley. I knocked on her door. I knew better than to just walk in. Sometimes every day was naked day for Aunt Shirley. Take my word on it.

"Who's there?"

"It's me," I whispered through the door. I didn't want Mom or Stella to overhear. "Do you have time to go over some theories?"

The door swung open. I was glad to see she was dressed in a bathrobe. She'd obviously washed the vile from her body, too. "Only if you go get me a drink. We drank all the tequila the other night, and your mom's being a pain and won't let me have anything before the rehearsal!"

Smart thinking on Mom's part. It's hard enough to predict Aunt Shirley when she's sober—nobody wanted to see a drunk Aunt Shirley at the wedding rehearsal.

"I'll go see what I can do. Grab paper and pen for when I get back."

I walked into the kitchen. On the island sat veggies, dips, and other yummy-looking appetizers. Mindy sat at the table sipping hot tea.

"Everything looks wonderful," I said and sat down across from her at the table.

She lowered her cup and smiled. "Thanks. We just finished up. It's been fun doing girl time with your mom and Stella. I can't remember when I've enjoyed myself so much. I'm almost sad to see it end."

"Me, too. Although I have to admit, I kinda miss the guys."

Mindy smiled. "Speaking of which, Hank said you better have something about the murders for him when he gets here tomorrow."

I rolled my eyes. "Yeah, yeah. Maybe I spoke too soon."

I got up from the table and snagged a bottle of white wine and two glasses. I knew Aunt Shirley would hate the fact I got her wine instead of tequila, but she was gonna have to live with it.

I opened her bedroom door and gently shut it behind me. I didn't want to alert too many people in the house as to what we were doing. Aunt Shirley was sitting on her bed still in her bathrobe.

"You wanna get dressed?" I asked, hoping she'd take the hint.

"Nope. Hand over the drink." She thrust her hand in my direction, and I pulled the wine up for her to see.

Aunt Shirley recoiled so fast she hit her head on the wall. "I don't want no *white wine.*"

I rolled my eyes. "Emphasizing every word? Really?"

"Well, *obviously* you didn't understand me when I said I wanted a drink. *Tequila* is a drink. White wine is something you have when you've lost a bet."

I shoved the glass in her hand. "Deal with it."

She took a tiny sip and shuddered.

Give me strength!

Aunt Shirley set aside her glass. "Let's brainstorm what we have so far."

"We have a syringe, which is used by both Whitney and Jolene, found at the crime scene," I said.

"Okay. But which one has the most to gain from the murders?" Aunt Shirley asked.

"Neither one," I said. "Jim was making Whitney a lot of money with his houses. She outsold Julie by a landslide. Killing Jim hurts her financially."

"But sometimes the heart does funny things. If she couldn't have him—and we all heard her say she didn't think Julie should have him—then she could have made sure no one else had him."

"What about Jolene?" I asked. "I mean as far as I can see, she gains nothing."

"Oh, but she has the best motive—revenge. Julie, herself, admitted Jolene hated and blamed her for some reason. And then when Julie's family took in Susie, I'd say Jolene totally lost it. She spent years in a psychiatric hospital just trying to deal with everything. Jealousy and hatred…both are excellent motives to kill."

"But why would Jolene kill Jim?"

"To make sure Julie hurt before she died?" Aunt Shirley mused. "Something along those lines."

I took another sip of my wine thinking about what she said. I knew from my previous dealings with psycho killers that pretty much anything could set them off to kill.

Aunt Shirley and I hashed out our theories a little longer, but we really didn't seem to be any closer to capturing the killer. We did, however, finish off the bottle of wine.

"Don't tell Mom I let you drink," I said. "She didn't want you drinking before the rehearsal."

"Don't worry," Aunt Shirley said. "She'll never know."

I was heading downstairs to fix my hair when my phone rang. I looked at the caller and my heart lurched.

"Hey, Garrett."

"Hey, Sin. Got your call. Good news on our end…we caught the guys doing the robberies late last night at a house in Granville. We finally got the last one to confess this afternoon."

Relief flooded me. Even though I know it's his job, I still get nervous when Garrett's on the job. And seeing as how he's the Chief of Police, he's always on the job. "That's great! I was beginning to get worried they'd never be caught. Congratulations."

"Thanks, babe. What about you? How'd it go down at the station today?"

I felt my eyes fill up with tears. I didn't want to be such a sissy, but I was really getting scared I'd be arrested soon. "Not good. Taggart really has it in for me. He all but said he'd be arresting me soon!"

I heard my breath catch on a sob and I wanted to kick myself. I didn't want Garrett to worry. "Do you want me to drive down tonight? Now that we've caught the bad guys, I can probably get away early."

"Don't be silly," I said. "You need to sleep. And the thing is, Taggart has no proof. It's not like he can get anything to stick to me. I haven't done anything!"

194

I bit my lip, wondering if I should tell Garrett what we'd done today at Julie's house and Jolene's trailer. Garrett usually hated it when I poked my nose into police business, even though it's what brought us together a couple months ago.

"What did you do?" Garrett sighed.

"What do you mean? How do you know I did anything?"

Garrett laughed. "You hesitated. What's up?"

I told him about going to Julie's house, which resulted in a lot of curse words. Then I told him about finding a syringe inside Julie's house, which resulted in even *more* curse words and shouts of "contaminating the crime scene," and "tampering with evidence." By the time I got to being at Jolene's trailer, I could hear him practically hyperventilating.

"You're going to get yourself thrown in jail for more than multiple murders if you don't stop breaking the law!"

I sighed. I don't know why I ever thought he'd take me seriously. "What Aunt Shirley and I discovered," I continued like I hadn't heard his hissy fit, "is that both Whitney and Jolene use syringes."

Silence.

"Maybe I'll drive down tonight," Garrett said. "See if Hank can leave in a few hours."

Even though I wanted him here with me, I knew it wasn't fair. "No, just wait until tomorrow. Go get some sleep. Besides, I'm sure Hank will be busy at the paper tonight anyway."

"Sin, please don't do anything crazy before I get there tomorrow."

I laughed. "I won't. I'm just going to town to get the flowers and a surprise for Paige and Matt," I assured him.

I heard a low chuckle. "Every time I turn around you seem to be in trouble."

I let out an exasperated breath. "That's not fair."

"I miss you, Sin."

I smiled. Even though he wanted to strangle me, he still missed me. That had to be a good sign.

"I miss you, too. I can't wait to see you tomorrow."

* * *

The rehearsal went off without a hitch. Paige's dad had arrived about an hour before the rehearsal, and his arrival changed the dynamics of everything for me. It somehow became more real that Paige was about to be married. Nothing would be the same anymore. I mean, she'd still be my best friend, but our days of hanging out and it just being the two of us would be no more. It'll always include Matt. And in a few years when babies started coming, it would always include kids.

I suddenly felt lonely. And even a little sorry for myself. While everyone was still in the living room, I sneaked off to the kitchen. Grabbing a jello shot left over from the other night, I downed one. Then another. Then another.

I was just beginning to feel a little better when Aunt Shirley strode in. Mom made sure Aunt Shirley looked respectable in a purple polyester pantsuit. With her new pink and purple hair color and purple pantsuit, she really did look nice. Setting her purse on the counter, Aunt Shirley grabbed one of the jello shots for herself.

"Mom will kill us if she catches us," I said.

Aunt Shirley laughed. "Doubtful."

196

Figuring she was right, I downed another shot. I eyed her cute purse. "Why did you bring a purse to the rehearsal?"

Aunt Shirley grinned and grabbed the purse. She tipped it on its side and twisted a cap I hadn't even seen. She then tipped it up to her mouth and took a long drink.

"Is your purse a flask?" I asked.

"You know it!" Aunt Shirley handed me the purse.

Jostling it up and down in my hand, I gauged the weight of the purse. It was pretty light, considering it held a pretty substantial amount of booze. Tipping the purse up to my mouth, I took a tiny swallow.

It took everything I had not to spit it back out. I'm not sure what I was expecting…wine, mixed drink, not sure. But straight Fireball Whisky wasn't it.

"Hey, you're not the only one without a man here tonight," Aunt Shirley scolded. "At least your man is coming up tomorrow. Old Man Jenkins couldn't come. So I'm ringing in the New Year alone. Don't judge me."

I shook my head to clear it. "I wouldn't think of it. Drink up, Auntie. Just don't let Mom see you."

Clutching the purse like a lifeline, Aunt Shirley took another nip at the purse.

I envied her.

"Come see how things turned out," Paige squealed as she slid into the kitchen. "It looks beautiful!"

Needing a little more liquid courage to get through the night, I grabbed the purse from Aunt Shirley and took a long swig.

Paige was right, the living room looked exquisite. The furniture had been pushed against the walls, and an ivory runner ran down the middle of the makeshift aisle. A few chairs were placed on either side of the aisle.

Megan and Mindy had painstakingly strung numerous strands of white Christmas lights from the ceiling and from one side of the wall to the other.

Everything looked amazing. The mantle would be decorated with the flowers I would pick up from the flower shop in the morning, along with our personal bouquets and boutonnieres. Everything was ready to go.

"It's been a long night," Mom said as she wrapped her arms through mine. "Your aunt is only slightly tipsy, the living room is all set up, and I've only cried ten times tonight. I'd say we're ready to have a wedding."

CHAPTER 24

"Wake up," Aunt Shirley hissed in my ear.

"What the heck," I groaned. "What're you doing, Aunt Shirley?"

"Shhh. You'll wake up Paige, and then we'll all be in trouble." She grabbed the covers and pulled them down. I immediately pulled them back up. "I've been thinking. I always do my best work when I'm tipsy. And I think we need to make a move on Whitney. The more I ponder it, the more I believe she's the one."

I groaned again and reached for my phone. It was two a.m. "What're you talking about?"

"Now's the time to strike. Or at least get a glimpse when she's least expecting it."

I sat up in bed, the covers pooling at my waist. I hated these moments. I knew she was right, but I also knew enough about Aunt Shirley to know somehow we were gonna end up in trouble.

"What do you propose?"

"Nothing crazy," Aunt Shirley said, pulling a black stocking cap over her colorful head. I barely refrained from laughing. The top of the hat sported a puffball. "Let's just sneak into town and look through her window. Nothing too crazy. Just a glimpse of her in her natural habitat."

Natural habitat? What was she…a baboon?

"Her natural habitat." I shook my head. I still wasn't convinced we could sneak out without anyone finding out. With Matt in the house, I knew our chances were slim.

"Don't worry about Matt and Nick," Aunt Shirley said, as though reading my mind. "They were pretty lit after the rehearsal dinner. They'll sleep like babies."

I bit my lip. I couldn't think of any other reason not to go. "Wait. We don't have an address."

Aunt Shirley chuckled. "Actually, we do. Remember when I went to the bathroom at Jim's office? Well, I happened to snap a couple pictures with my phone of his Rolodex. I didn't know people still used those things."

I sighed. "Okay, let's do this."

I dressed in dark sweats and sweatshirt, threw a cap over my head, and tiptoed up the stairs as quietly as I could. Aunt Shirley was waiting for me in the kitchen.

I grabbed my keys and we slunk out to the Falcon. Luckily I'd parked the Falcon as far away from the house as possible when we came home from our errands that afternoon. Praying no one would hear, I drove us into town.

Aunt Shirley plugged in the address on her phone and a male, Australian accent led us toward Whitney's.

"Seriously?" I asked.

Aunt Shirley grinned. "He sounds yummy."

I found Whitney's house without too much trouble. It was a beautiful, one-story brick house with lots of windows, doors, and tiny pitched roofs in the front. It smacked of money. No surprise there.

I parked two houses down from Whitney's and turned off the Falcon. Putting on our gloves, we walked briskly to the front of the house. Our breath came out in tiny puffs of smoke.

"Looks like a light is on in the house," Aunt Shirley said. We parted the bushes underneath one of the windows and peered inside. A faint glow of a flickering TV illuminated the back room.

"Must be the living room," I said.

"We're never going to see anything from out here. We need inside."

Snippets of my earlier conversation with Garrett floated through my mind. "Absolutely not! It's one thing to peep in on someone without them knowing. It's a felony to enter their house."

Aunt Shirley rolled her eyes. "Don't go soft on me now, girl. We need inside. Unless you *want* to be arrested tomorrow and spend out the rest of your life in jail."

I knew she was goading me—trying to get under my skin. It worked. "Fine."

"Good, girl. Let's just see if there's anything open on the side here."

I grabbed Aunt Shirley's arm as she turned to walk away. "What if there's an alarm?"

Aunt Shirley snorted. "This girl is so narcissistic. She's not going to have an alarm. She believes she's above everyone and no one would dare enter her house, much less enter to hurt her."

I bit my lip and stewed. Usually Aunt Shirley was right about these things. I sighed and followed her as she crossed in front of the two-car garage and around the corner of the house. There was a side door leading into the garage.

Aunt Shirley carefully twisted the knob and pushed. The door swung open. We crossed the threshold and entered the dark garage. I pulled off my gloves, dug out my phone, and hit the flashlight app. Light illuminated the garage.

We carefully stepped over the debris on the garage floor. Another door on the opposite side of the garage led to the interior of the house. I knew if I went in, I'd be breaking the promise I made to myself to never break and enter into a house again with Aunt Shirley. That promise lasted all of a day.

Aunt Shirley stopped in front of the door and put a finger to her lips. Like she needed to tell me to keep my mouth shut. I almost laughed out loud at that ridiculous notion.

Praying nothing would go wrong, I shut off the flashlight app and followed Aunt Shirley into the house. We entered a small laundry room that spilled into the kitchen. Our running shoes glided silently across the tile flooring.

"Look through the drawers," Aunt Shirley whispered, "and see if you can find a knife. Anything that might lead to the murder weapon at Julie's."

She started at one end of the kitchen and I went to the other. We silently opened countless drawers. I wasn't sure what to look for. I had no idea what kind of knife was used. Was it a serrated, butcher, or what?

I found a drawer with about seven knives and motioned for Aunt Shirley. She gently picked up a couple and twisted them in the moonlight. I assumed she was looking for blood.

A huge rounded archway to the left led into the living room. Whitney was softly snoring on the couch in front of the TV.

I'm thinking the two empty wine bottles on the coffee table were helpful in her recent coma-like state. There was a little red wine left in a clear, deep-set glass. An empty syringe lay next to the wine glass and bottle of insulin.

Aunt Shirley put two fingers up to her eyes and then pointed them down the hall. She then tapped on her wrist with the other hand.

Now she fancies herself a SWAT leader?

"What?" I mouthed angrily to her.

"You take the rooms on the left. I'll take the rooms on the right."

Splitting up did not sound like a good idea at all. Before I could say anything, Aunt Shirley took off down the darkened hallway. She opened a door and slipped inside.

Knowing I was in too deep to back out, I hurried down the hallway and opened the first door on my left, sliding into the room. It looked like an extra bedroom. Moonlight shone through the window, and I waited for my eyes to adjust.

On the wall were pictures of Jim. I walked over to them. It looked like Whitney had thumbtacked them haphazardly into the wall. I leaned in and could make out Jim looking over his shoulder and laughing at someone while he carried a piece of drywall. There were countless pictures scattered across the walls. The eerie thing was, in most of them he appeared unaware that he was being photographed. Sometimes he was bent over a saw or outside looking at the front of a house.

I walked the length of the wall, silently looking at the pictures. I stopped in front of one that had Jim with his arm around

Julie. Or at least I'm assuming it was Julie. All I could make out was her body—the face had been scratched out with a pen.

I turned and caught my breath. On the closet door hung a picture of Julie's face. Darts were embedded in her forehead and chin.

Whimpering, I quickly raced to the door. The sooner I got out of the room the better. I quietly opened the door, only to hear a toilet flush.

Was Whitney up?

Before I could duck back into the room, the door opened and out came Aunt Shirley.

"Did you pee in there?" I hissed.

"Yep."

I was about to chew her out when movement to my right caught my attention. A pair of eyes seemed to be floating in the pitch-black hallway.

"Uh oh," Aunt Shirley whispered. A piercing scream echoed the hallway, and a black cat jumped on Aunt Shirley's parka, clawing its way up to her head.

"Mr. Savage," Whitney's drunken voice yelled out. "Is that you? What's wrong baby?"

Aunt Shirley and I bolted down the hallway, rounding the corner as Whitney stumbled into the unlit hall behind us. I glanced back and saw Mr. Savage holding on tightly to Aunt Shirley's head, while simultaneously batting at the puffball on top of the hat.

I yanked open a door on my right and we staggered inside. We could hear Whitney calling for Mr. Savage the whole time. I pushed Aunt Shirley toward the closet. She reached up and yanked

204

Mr. Savage off her head, the cap going with the cat. He howled his outrage at being thrown down on the bed.

I pushed Aunt Shirley through the bi-fold closet doors and quietly closed the doors as much as I could. We both took deep breaths to try and stop our panting. The closet doors were open enough that if Whitney looked hard, she'd see us huddled in the closet.

"Mr. Savage, are you in here?" Whitney stumbled into the bedroom, setting her wine glass down on the dresser.

Mr. Savage was still hissing his outrage at being dumped onto the bed.

"What's the matter, baby? You want your mommy?" Whitney collapsed onto the bed next to the hat-clutching cat. Mr. Savage jumped off the bed, hat still clutched in his paws.

"Night," Whitney mumbled right before she passed out.

We waited a few more minutes in silence. It was the longest three minutes of my life. Once again I cursed Aunt Shirley as I tried to control my breathing.

"Let's go," Aunt Shirley hissed in my ear. Her brightly colored hair was sticking up all over her head.

I gently pushed one side of the bi-fold closet doors open. Turning sideways I eased out of the closet, Aunt Shirley following close behind. Mr. Savage stopped batting the puffball around when he saw us. Black yarn was strewn all over the room.

It was a standoff.

Aunt Shirley won when she reached down and grabbed her cap off the floor. Mr. Savage hissed and swatted Aunt Shirley's hand with his paw.

I grabbed onto Aunt Shirley's parka and pulled her through the bedroom door. We slunk back through the house and out the garage door. Turning on my flashlight app we made our way quickly to the Falcon.

I rested my head against the steering wheel and waited until I stopped shaking.

"Stupid cat ruined my hat!" I looked over at Aunt Shirley. She was wiggling the now poofless hat. "My ball is gone."

I chortled. "One thing you got, it's plenty of balls."

Aunt Shirley grinned at me. "I like that."

Shaking my head I started the Falcon. The low purr of the car helped sooth my nerves.

I told Aunt Shirley what I saw in the extra bedroom. About the secretly obtained pictures and the dartboard of Julie.

"I'm not sure that's guilt," Aunt Shirley said, "since it's mostly circumstantial evidence. But it at least puts a shadow over her."

"So did this crazy excursion get us any closer to proving Whitney the murderer?" I asked.

Aunt Shirley thought a moment. "Like I said, it's all circumstantial. The syringe, the pictures and dartboard, the obvious hatred of Julie because of Jim. But no direct evidence. We have no way of linking Whitney to the drill at Jim's place or the knife from Julie's murder."

"But we can agree she's moved up on the list of suspects?"

Aunt Shirley nodded. "You bet."

CHAPTER 25

"Thanks for coming with me," I said to Aunt Shirley as we piled into the Falcon and headed into town to pick up the flowers and help Susie with the archway. We were actually way ahead of schedule.

I was glad to be getting out of the house. People were starting to stress out with the ceremony only a few hours away. I'd just finished taking pictures of Paige and Matt in the gazebo with the snow-covered branches and crystalized lake in the background.

Most people are superstitious and don't want to see the bride or groom before the wedding—but Paige wanted stellar pictures. She had her hair, makeup, and wedding dress on by ten o'clock ready to smile for the camera. Matt looked dapper in his charcoal suit and pale pink tie to match my bridesmaid dress.

The pictures didn't take long, and before we'd left, Paige was back in her sweats helping with last-minute food and drink preparations.

"I'm just glad everyone else decided to stay behind," Aunt Shirley said.

"Me, too. I need some time to clear my mind and figure out our next move."

"I think we should drive by Jim's shop in town and just see if Amber Leigh is there. I think it's time to ask her if she knows anything about the syringe. If she doesn't, I say we cross her off the list for sure."

"Today?" I asked incredulously. "If we're late, Paige and Mom will *kill* us!"

"Don't worry, I have it all under control. Plus, we need to take a little extra time. I'm dying to try out the Christmas present I bought me. I've been surrounded by people all week…no alone time."

I jerked my head in her direction. "Tell me you didn't bring the gun."

Aunt Shirley squinted up her face disapprovingly. "No, I didn't bring the gun. I brought *this* instead!" She whipped out a long, skinny tube and a small tackle box from inside her camo parka.

"Is that some kind of fishing thing?" I asked. "It's a little cold to be fishing."

Aunt Shirley snickered. "It's a blowgun with darts, you ninny."

I turned left and stopped in front of the flower shop. Their lights were off, so I hunkered down to wait.

"Let me show you what she can do," Aunt Shirley said excitedly. She opened the car door and motioned for me to follow her.

I sighed, turned off the Falcon, and followed her down the street to the city park. Not surprising, there wasn't a single person in the park.

"See that tree over there," Aunt Shirley said and pointed to a spot about twenty yards away. "I'm going to hit it with this dart."

She put a tiny dart into the tube then lifted it to her mouth. The dart flew out of the end of the tube…and landed with a *thwack*! on the bench next to the tree.

"So my aim's a little off," Aunt Shirley said, jogging to retrieve the dart.

"You know how much I hate anything related to darts after what happened to me a few months ago. Why did you buy that?"

"Well, your Barney Fife boyfriend won't stop hounding me about my gun, so I thought this might come in handy."

"He'll arrest you if he hears you call him Barney Fife," I said smugly as she put the tube and tackle box back inside her camouflage parka.

"Doesn't look like the flower shop is going to open early," Aunt Shirley mused. "How about you drive on out to Jim's business? Let's see if Amber Leigh is out there."

It didn't take long to get to Jim's place. We were lucky enough to see Amber Leigh coming out of the office, stopping to lock the door. From the look of things, she'd been packing up.

"Hey, Amber Leigh," I called out from the Falcon's window.

Amber Leigh screamed and whirled around. "You scared me! What do you want?"

"I just want to ask you a quick question," I said. "What are you doing?"

"That's your question?" Amber Leigh raged. "You want to know what I'm doing?"

"Um…no. I have a different question. I was just being friendly and asking what you were doing here on a Sunday morning moving out boxes." Okay, I probably could have said it a little nicer, but I didn't like her attitude.

Aunt Shirley and I got out and walked over to where Amber Leigh was standing.

"Not that it's any of your business," Amber Leigh said, "but Josh wants to finish the jobs. No way am I sticking around and working for a kid."

Aunt Shirley peeked into the open box. "Still doesn't explain why you're taking files out of the office."

Amber Leigh glared at us. "None of your business. These are my leads. Josh is on his own."

I frowned at her. "I don't think legally you can take files out of a business that isn't yours. I believe they call that stealing."

Amber Leigh huffed. "What do you want?"

I shoved my hands into my pockets to help keep them warm. "We came by to see if you have diabetes or take insulin?"

"What? Why?"

Now I was just thinking on the fly. I didn't know she'd question me. "Because we found a bottle the other day out here. And we figured it must be pretty expensive, so we wanted to give it to the owner." I thought it sounded plausible.

Amber Leigh shifted the box to her other hip, obviously irritated. "No, I don't have diabetes or take insulin shots. Happy now?"

Aunt Shirley snorted. "I won't be happy until I wake up one morning without any aches or pains."

We trekked back to the Falcon and headed back into town.

"Well, I guess that takes care of that," Aunt Shirley said. "We can scratch her off the list. I think I'll call Josh and let him know what's going on over there."

"You have his number?"

Aunt Shirley grinned. "I pocketed some of Jim's business cards the other day when we were inside. They also list Josh's number.

Aunt Shirley dialed the number on the card and told Josh what was going on at Jim's office.

"He's on his way over. I hope she doesn't take much," Aunt Shirley said as she dropped the phone into her purse.

The flower shop was open when we arrived. Two people were inside answering the phone and taking orders. It was awful busy…which was understandable seeing as how in one week there were two deaths.

The owner ran over to us. "We are breaking our rule about not opening on Sundays. With this second murder, our orders for funeral flowers are numerous. We'll never get everything done if we don't work today."

"Have you heard anything more?" I asked. I hoped she didn't say I was the number one suspect.

"Not really," she said, biting her lip nervously. "We're all so scared that we decided to work in pairs today. No one is to be left alone in the shop."

"I'm sure you have nothing to worry about," I assured her.

Suspicion had her giving me the eye. "Why do you say that?" The store owner took a step backward and looked over her shoulder at the young girl on the phone taking orders.

"No, no," I said quickly. "I just mean it's unlikely that…" I trailed off. I didn't know what to say without making me seem suspicious.

"Statistically speaking, the chances of another murder happening are slim," Aunt Shirley said.

The shop owner still looked uncertain. But I guess human nature being what it is she didn't want to ask too many questions for fear of the answers.

The young girl on the phone taking orders hung up and walked over to us. She was your typical high school kid—long, flowing hair, thin and curvy at the same time. She had beautiful green eyes with a few freckles scattered across her nose.

"Hi. My name's Annabel. I kind of eavesdropped on your conversation. It's so sad what's happened. I've talked to a lot of my friends from school, and we're all in shock."

"How so?" Aunt Shirley asked.

Annabel chewed on her lower lip. "Well, a lot of kids are saying that Josh is responsible. That he killed Jim and Julie. Of course, I keep telling my friends Josh couldn't have done this. I mean, he's so nice and cute."

It took all my effort not to laugh. I didn't want to insult her. I also didn't have the heart to crush her innocence by telling her being cute wasn't a good enough alibi for the police.

"I have heard, though, that he's kinda taking over right now since Jim's dead. So maybe that's why he did it?" Annabel shrugged.

"If he only wanted the business, there'd be no reason to kill Julie," Aunt Shirley informed Annabel.

"You're right," Annabel said. "I don't think Josh had anything to do with it. I just hope the kids at school don't harass him too much if the killer isn't caught by the time we get back to school."

Me, too. That's the last thing he needs.

"By the way," Annabel said to Aunt Shirley, "Rocking the hair!"

Aunt Shirley grinned and patted her colorful curls. She'd decided to wear her normally straight hair curly for the wedding, which really made her colors pop.

"Thanks," Aunt Shirley said.

It didn't take long to load the flowers into the backseat of the Falcon. I decided to text Garrett to see where he and Hank were.

"Picked up the flowers. Heading to Susie's house 2 get a surprise 4 Paige. Don't tell her. Where R U?"

Less than a minute later I got a reply text from Garrett. "Pulling into lake house right now. Hurry home...missed u!"

I felt a silly grin spread over my face. "Should be back at lake house in 15 minutes. Missed U 2."

Feeling giddy, I slipped the phone back into my pocket and steered the Falcon toward Susie's house. I'd already pulled her address up on my navigation app, so I knew where to go.

Unlike Julie, Susie bought a house closer to the lake. It was definitely in a newer section of homes. If I remembered correctly, when we were kids, this area used to be where the old hospital clinic was. We pulled into a cul-de-sac. With only three houses on the street, it offered seclusion, a private dock to the lake, and spectacular views.

A new home and a new business. Her parents must have had one heck of a life insurance policy.

"How do you think she affords all this?" I asked Aunt Shirley as we parked in the cobblestone driveway and got out of the Falcon. It was almost identical to Whitney's house. Brick, lots of windows, numerous pitched roofs.

"Don't know. I guess she'd have gotten money from both the fire insurance and the life insurance policies."

I suddenly felt guilty for envying Susie. No amount of money would be worth losing my family over.

Aunt Shirley and I carefully made our way up the cobblestone walkway toward the front of the house. I was just about to ring the bell when the back gate opened and Susie popped her head out.

"Right on time, Ryli," Susie called cheerfully. "Oh, hello Aunt Shirley. I wasn't expecting you, too."

Aunt Shirley and I peered around the corner and waved.

"Come on back and help me load the archway if you don't mind. I have the cake already loaded up and ready to go. It looks fabulous!"

Aunt Shirley and I walked around the house and through the fence. It was odd she'd put a fence up around the house, because now she had to open it to go down to her private dock.

"I know it seems weird putting a fence up," Susie said, as though she'd read my mind, "but Jim talked me into putting a little shed back here for my business. It's temperature controlled and has electricity. Before I set up shop downtown, this is where I baked and housed my goods. I felt I needed some privacy because of the expensive items I had to have back here."

Susie stopped talking when she came to the door of the beige shed. "You didn't tell me how things were going this morning. Is everyone ready for the ceremony?" Susie asked.

"Yep. I took some pictures this morning of Paige and Matt in their wedding attire. The natural lighting was perfect."

"I love your hair up like that," Susie said.

214

I patted my Dutch braid. I was ecstatic at how it came out. "Thanks."

Susie swung open the door and motioned Aunt Shirley and me to go on in.

"I'm so glad to hear everything's ready," Susie said as she closed the door behind us. "It seems to be coming together on my end, too."

I'm not sure what I was expecting, but the poorly lit room and serial killer-like plastic all over the place definitely wasn't it.

Aunt Shirley and I walked farther into the room. I let out a yelp when I saw Jolene sprawled out on a metal table, obviously high as a kite, a needle haphazardly next to her.

Aunt Shirley was just as shocked. "What the—"

She didn't finish her sentence. Instead, Aunt Shirley crumpled to the ground in a huge, camouflage heap. It'd happened so fast, I didn't even see it coming.

I dropped to the ground next to Aunt Shirley to check on her. My hands were shaking as I pushed the hood back to see her face. Blood was running down her head. I wasn't sure if it was from the blow Susie gave her or from hitting her head on the cement when she went down.

"That's for talking smack about my healthy bread the other day, you old cow. Get up, Ryli," Susie ordered, waving around the gun she'd hit Aunt Shirley with. "She's fine. I just gave her a tap, that's all."

I looked up at Susie, so filled with rage I couldn't see straight. I guess she must have guessed my intent, because she jabbed the gun against my forehead.

"I said get up!" Spittle flew from Susie's mouth.

I was trying to stay calm. I couldn't get my body to comply with her orders, so she yanked me up herself...the whole time keeping the gun aimed at me.

"I don't understand," I said. I hated the tremor in my voice. I didn't want her to know how scared I really was.

"Of course you don't, Ryli," Susie sneered and pushed me toward the middle of the room. The clear plastic crunched beneath my feet as she led me over to a workbench on the other side of the room. As I passed by Jolene, I couldn't help but check to see if she was still breathing.

She was.

"Put your hands together," Susie demanded as she snatched up some rope off the workbench. I was trying to come up with a plan to get us out of this mess, but nothing was coming to me. Susie stuck the gun in her waistband and proceeded to tie my hands together.

CHAPTER 26

I looked over at Aunt Shirley again. She still hadn't moved.

Susie finished tying me up, pulled the gun back out of her pants, and motioned for me to sit on the wooden barstool next to the workbench.

I sat down and silently watched as Susie went to stand by Jolene. She tucked the gun back into her pants. In the blink of an eye, Susie slapped Jolene across the face with her open palm. Jolene moaned but didn't open her eyes.

"You've always been a worthless sister," Susie sneered. "I guess I'll have to do this all on my own, then blame it on you like I did our parents' death."

I jerked my head up.

Had Susie just confessed to killing her parents? If I managed to get us out of this alive, Hank was gonna give me a huge promotion with the story I was going to give him.

"Why did you kill your parents?" I asked.

Susie glared at me. "Shut up, Ryli. I'll get to you after I take care of your nosey aunt."

My heart dropped to my stomach. I couldn't let her kill Aunt Shirley. I pushed myself up from the barstool. "Please don't hurt her."

Susie whipped out the gun and pointed it at me. "Don't even think of moving. Sit back down." Susie walked backward toward Aunt Shirley.

Susie stared hatefully down at Aunt Shirley, who was still out cold. She reached down and yanked Aunt Shirley's arms up and started dragging Aunt Shirley across the cement floor.

"Jeez, old lady" Susie said, pausing to wipe sweat from her brow, "lose some weight. It's like dragging cement sacks."

I prayed Aunt Shirley didn't wake up and hear Susie. Aunt Shirley would go postal on Susie, which would definitely end with Aunt Shirley being shot.

Susie opened a door I hadn't noticed at the back of the shed. She tugged Aunt Shirley's unconscious body inside the room.

Jumping up from my seat, I frantically searched for the cell phone in my pocket. I'd heard it vibrate twice in the last two minutes. I knew it had to be Garrett, worried why I wasn't back yet. I just didn't know how to let him know where I was.

I started whimpering when I realized my hands were too tightly bound to reach into my pocket and retrieve my cell. Trying not to let panic set in, I tried to think of a way to stall Susie.

"I told you to sit down!" Susie screamed as she hurried back into the room.

"Where's Aunt Shirley?" I demanded.

"In the shower. I figure after I kill you, I can just shoot her in the shower and let the blood drain out. No mess to clean up. So practical...so practical," Susie sang as she went to stand near Jolene.

I felt my pocket vibrate again. Time to stall until I could come up with a way to let Garrett know where I was.

"Okay, I give. Why did you do all this?"

Susie's hate-filled eyes locked on me. She hit Jolene upside the head again. "Do you know what it's like to grow up with a sister addicted to drugs? A sister that will give herself to any guy that will give her something for free?"

I wasn't exactly sure if that was a rhetorical question or not. "No."

Susie laughed bitterly. "All my life I grew up with this messed up piece of trash for a sister. Every time she'd get in trouble, my parents would come down harder on *me*! I never did anything wrong, because I wasn't allowed to do anything!"

A light was beginning to come on...but I didn't know how Jolene's pathetic life led to Julie and Jim having to die.

Susie picked up a knife lying near the table. "The night before I killed my parents, they told me they didn't want me going to my senior prom. They said since Jolene had managed to get in trouble with the law that night by getting high, leaving the dance, and then getting into a car wreck, that somehow *I* might fall into that same routine. *Me!*"

I watched in horror as the knife accidentally nicked Susie under her chin when she pointed to herself.

"You know those moments of clarity some people say they have?" Susie asked. "That's what it was for me. I knew all I had to do was get Jolene high as a kite, set the fire, and watch her take the blame."

Tapping the blade against Jolene's head, Susie continued, "But that worthless Taggart couldn't make anything stick to you, could he my little meth head? Nope. No matter how many lies I told about seeing Jolene going to my parents' room that night, about her being mad they took her drug stash away, the threats she supposedly made…he let her walk!"

Susie slapped Jolene again. This time Jolene moaned and tried to open her eyes.

"I thought getting rid of my parents would make things easier for me. But no, I had to stay with Julie and her strict parents until I turned eighteen and the insurance kicked in."

"Susie," Jolene moaned hoarsely, "what's going on?"

"Nothing you need to worry your pathetic little meth head over," Susie sneered down at her sister.

"Okay." Taking Susie at her word, Jolene closed her eyes and fell blissfully into a drug-induced sleep.

"Disgusting, isn't she?" Susie asked.

"But you never said why you killed Jim and Julie. What did they ever do to you? I mean, Julie took you in when—well, after you cold-bloodedly murdered your parents." I knew I probably shouldn't taunt her, but I couldn't seem to help myself.

"You think I wanted to go live with her? I couldn't wait to get away from that pathetic loser. I hated her as much as Whitney did. I couldn't wait to get out of this town and away from everything here."

I tried to stay focused on her confession, but my mind kept trying to formulate an escape plan.

"I'd made some sound investments with the money I got from the insurance company. So when I came back to Cavern Beach, money in hand, Jim was so helpful in building me a house. Then he helped me renovate the bakery in town. We were spending so much time together…" Susie trailed off, looking into space. "I'd listen to Whitney go on and on about how she thought Jim was in love with *her* because they spent so much time together building and selling houses. She's so delusional!"

Pot meet kettle...kettle meet pot.

"Then one morning Julie stopped by the bakery. She said it was just to say hi and ask Jim a question about one of his houses she was trying to sell. But I could see she was jealous of how much time Jim was spending with me. That fat cow could protest all she wanted...I knew better!"

Déjà vu all over again. Now comes the crazy killer spouting wacked out beliefs.

A shadow passed in front of the shed's door. Had Garrett found me already? I hadn't even texted him yet!

"The night I went out to Jim's house—the night you all had your drunken party—I didn't go out there to kill him." Susie wiped a tear with the back of her knife-clenching fist. "I just went out there to tell him how I felt. To tell him I cared about him. That he didn't have to seek solace in a worthless nobody like Julie. And do you know what he said?" Spittle once again started flying out of her mouth. "He said he was only being nice to me because *he* felt sorry for *me!*"

Touchdown! We've officially reached crazy town!

"When he said that...well, I just saw red. Luckily the drill just happened to be sitting on his work bench. He's still going on and on about how he wants me to leave and never come back. I grabbed the drill and made a run at him." Susie laughed. "He was so surprised. He didn't know what hit him!"

My stomach rolled and pitched. It was all I could do not to throw up.

"And that's when I realized I could kill Julie and make it look like Whitney or Jolene did it. I didn't care which one got arrested. When I killed Julie, I made sure to drop a syringe I knew both of them used." Still clutching the knife, Susie lifted her fist and hit herself repeatedly in the temple. "But once again that worthless Taggart couldn't find a body in a body bag, and he totally missed the clue I planted!"

"Until we found it."

Susie giggled. "That must be why Whitney called me last night spouting off about you and your crazy aunt accusing her of murder. Oh, I wish I could have seen her face when you accused her."

The door to the shed quietly slid open. Since Susie had her back to the shed door, she couldn't see Garrett and Hank as they crept in. I tried to make my face as blank as possible. I didn't want to give their position away.

Susie sighed and put the knife on the table. "But now things have gotten so complicated. Jolene has outlived her usefulness." Susie reached down and tried to lift Jolene into a sitting position, slapping her repeatedly in the face.

"What?" mumbled Jolene, trying to open her eyes.

"Dear sister," Susie crooned, "I have one more job for you to do for me."

Jolene's head flopped around on her neck. "Where is he? Will he give me something to make me feel better when I'm done?"

"You bet. All he wants you to do is hold this gun and aim it over there. Once you pull the trigger, you can have all the drugs you want."

The spit in my mouth dried up. I couldn't help it when my eyes darted wildly to Garrett. Seeing my look, Susie quickly grabbed the gun from Jolene and pointed it at Garrett.

I screamed and jumped up off the barstool and took off after her. She pivoted, throwing Jolene off the metal table. Jolene's head hit the floor with a sickening thud. That momentarily stopped me in my tracks. I couldn't see where Jolene had fallen, but I could see blood starting to pool on the floor.

"Stay right there," Susie yelled, pointing the gun between Garrett, Hank, and me. Without even looking at her sister, she walked over to where I was standing at pressed the gun against my temple.

"Let's talk this out," Garrett said as he lowered his gun a little.

Why are you lowering your gun? Shoot her! Shoot her!

"There's nothing to talk about anymore. I'm going to shoot your girlfriend, shoot you, shoot him, and then go inside that bathroom and shoot that pain-in-the-butt aunt of hers," Susie ranted. "Thank God I placed all this plastic around. I'd have a devil of a time getting all these blood stains out."

Susie was still rambling on when I saw Hank's eyes go wide as he slapped his neck in pain. "What the—"

That was enough to jar Susie from her rantings. Turning me with her toward the back of the room, Aunt Shirley was standing in the open doorway. Before I could scream at Aunt Shirley to run, she lifted the blowgun to her mouth and shot again.

This time she hit her mark.

Sort of.

The dart landed in Susie's eye.

Screaming in pain, Susie dropped the gun from my head and bent over. "My eye! My eye! I'll kill you slowly!" She went to stand back up. Without even thinking, I swung my rope-bound hands as hard as I could at her head. I caught the dart in her eye with the back of my hand.

Susie dropped to the floor like a lead balloon. My first thought was I'd killed her. I looked up as Aunt Shirley came running toward me, shoving the blowgun back inside her parka.

My knees buckled. I'd have gone down too if it hadn't been for Garrett catching me. "You scared me to death!" He rocked me back and forth in his arms.

I could see Hank over Garrett's shoulder. He was cursing and trying to yank the dart out of his neck.

I heard sirens in the background. "It's about time," Garrett muttered. "I told that sorry Chief to get down here ten minutes ago!"

"How—how did you know where I was?" I stuttered. Unfortunately, I knew from past experience my body was going into shock.

Garrett laughed. "Are you forgetting about the tracking app I put in your phone?"

I pulled back from him, narrowing my eyes. "You never told me you put a tracking device on my phone!"

"I didn't? Hmmm…must have slipped my mind."

I slapped his arm. "I can't believe you're tracking my every move. That's so stalker like!"

Garrett leaned in and kissed me. "No. That's what a guy has to do when he dates a murder-magnet like yourself. Seems every time I turn my back, someone is trying to kill you."

Seeing as how he was right, I let it go.

For now.

"And you," Garrett said, pointing at Aunt Shirley. "Where did you get that thing?"

Aunt Shirley laughed. "Got me a new blowgun for Christmas."

Garrett shook his head then pulled me close. "I missed you." He gently kissed me again.

"What is it with you two crazy women and darts to the neck?" Hank grumbled. "How many times can you use that trick?"

I started to giggle against Garrett's lips. Hank was right. It seems there's always a dart to the neck whenever I'm involved.

"Hold it right there," Chief Taggard demanded. "Put your hands in the air!"

I opened my eyes and looked over Garrett's shoulder to see Chief Taggart charging through the door, his gun drawn. "I said get your hands in the air!"

Garrett tucked me under his arm. "Taggart," he growled, "I'm going to give you three seconds to stop pointing that gun at my girlfriend before I physically remove it from you and make you eat it."

I giggled again. I couldn't help it. Garrett managed to say the very thing I was thinking.

"Hey, look here what I found," Aunt Shirley hollered.

I got up and walked over to where she was standing. Inside the refrigerator was Paige's wedding cake. The dark pink ribbon made the tiny cake pop. And the extra touch of edible snowflakes elevated it to stunning. Just like Susie said it would.

"Do you think we should take it?" I asked. I was a little unsure if it was healthy. "Do you think she poisoned it?"

"If she wanted to take us out with food, she'd have done it at the bachelorette party. As whackadoo as she is, I think Susie honestly believed in her craft. I don't think she'd risk it or her bakery's reputation."

I bit my lower lip. Deciding to roll the dice, I reached down and grabbed the cake from the refrigerator. This was still going to be Paige's special day.

CHAPTER 27

By the time everything was sorted out, we'd missed the two o'clock timeline for the wedding. It took a few hours to give countless statements over and over again, watch the ambulance carry Jolene's dead body out in a body bag, and watch as the EMTs tried to save Susie's eye. Doc Powell said it was pointless. The eye was a goner.

When Garrett and Hank hadn't come back from searching for us, everyone back at the house had piled into cars and went looking for us. Luckily Nick had a police scanner app downloaded on his phone, so he heard the 911 call Garrett had placed to Chief Taggart. Since Cavern Beach is such a small town, they just followed the cop cars and ambulance through town to where Aunt Shirley and I were being held.

I have to admit, seeing Hank get shot in the neck with a dart brought back a lot of scary memories for me. If I ever saw another dart again, it would be too soon.

Garrett must have known I was having flashbacks, because he didn't lecture me near as much as he could have on the way back to the lake house. He did do a lot of yelling at Aunt Shirley, but she could take it.

Paige and Megan had stayed back at the house when everyone else left to go into town to try and find us. They were to keep the preacher and his wife entertained so they wouldn't leave.

As everyone took turns carrying in the flowers from the backseat of the Falcon, I went downstairs to get ready for the wedding.

I'd just taken my bridesmaid dress out of the closet when my bedroom door opened. In rushed Mom and Paige, hugging me again at the same time.

"Careful of the dress," I hollered as I held the dress out of reach. And while I appreciated the fact they were so happy to see me, Mom had done this twenty times during the two hours we were at the crime scene.

"Don't *ever* scare me like that again!" Mom said as she wiped tears from her eyes. "I'm getting too old to deal with this. This is the second time in three months I have to hear about you taking out a murderer."

"I didn't take this one out," I said. "Aunt Shirley did."

I could tell Mom wasn't impressed with my wit.

"I'm not kidding," Mom scolded. "I've gotten used to having to worry about your brother with the jobs he's always had—military, fireman, EMT, and now soon as a police officer. I shouldn't have to worry about you, my only daughter."

She almost knew just how to guilt me into obedience. "Don't be sexist, Mom," I grinned. "Matt shouldn't have all the fun."

Mom swatted me and then walked out the door without another word.

Paige smiled. "Stop giving your mom fits. She really was worried when we realized something was wrong."

Guilt again. This time it worked. "I'll try not to. I don't know why, but trouble just seems to follow me wherever I go."

"We've been best friends longer than I can remember. You aren't telling me anything I don't know. Now, let's get you in this dress so I can marry the man of my dreams."

* * *

A few hours and two glasses of wine later, I was standing out on the back deck looking down at the semi-frozen lake. I refused to take off my bridesmaid dress and shawl. I felt too beautiful.

I tipped back my head and swallowed loudly. Nothing like a gun to the head to make you want to drink your worries away.

"I thought I'd find you out here," Garrett said as he closed the door behind him. He wrapped me in his arms, warming me instantly.

I rested my head on his chest. I loved hearing his heart thump against my ear. It made me feel safe…protected.

He kissed me on top of my head. "What's wrong?"

"I'm so happy for Paige and Matt. Yet I can't help but be sad how this week ended up. All these deaths were so senseless."

"Murders usually are," Garrett said softly.

I knew he was trying to make me feel better, but he wasn't helping. "Happy New Year," I whispered, standing on my tiptoes to give him a kiss.

We stayed like that for a while, kissing and necking on the back deck. Just when I was about to make a more aggressive move, the door opened and out stumbled Aunt Shirley.

"You youngins…always so eager to make out," she scoffed.

I laughed, hugging Garrett to me. "Please, if Old Man Jenkins was here, you'd be all over him."

"You're probably right," Aunt Shirley cackled.

"Did you need something, Aunt Shirley?" Garrett asked in an intimidating voice. I guess he was hoping she'd take the hint and leave us in peace.

"Nope," Aunt Shirley said and pulled out her electric cigarette for a few puffs. She jammed it back in her pocket and turned to leave. "Oh, by the way, I thought you guys might be interested to know I've been hired for a job. Investigation work."

Garrett set me aside and pointed his finger at Aunt Shirley. "Now listen here. There's no way you're going back into the field. You have to be licensed to be a private investigator, and I know for a fact you're not. By law I would have to report you."

"Simmer down, Ace," Aunt Shirley taunted Garrett. "I'm not giving you a run for your money just yet."

I reached up and grabbed his arms. "Don't kill her on Paige and Matt's wedding day, please. It'd put a black mark on the day." I turned to her. "What's this job?"

Aunt Shirley looked inside the house and withdrew the bottle of tequila she'd stashed in her coat. Saluting Hank inside the house, she took a swig. He grinned back.

"Seems I've been hired as an investigative journalist to work at the *Gazette* with you, Ryli," Aunt Shirley said, putting the bottle back in her coat pocket.

"No way did Hank hire you!" I squinted at Hank through the French doors inside the house.

Hank must have been able to read my lips, because he nodded and walked toward the kitchen...laughing the whole time.

"Looks like you and me are gonna be a regular Cagney and Lacey team," Aunt Shirley said. "I already got some ideas where we can start."

230

Garrett growled.

"Cagney and Lacey were cops, Aunt Shirley," I said quickly. "We aren't cops. We're reporters."

"That's what you think," Aunt Shirley said.

"Now look here," Garrett started in…but he never got to finish. Instead, Aunt Shirley winked at me and walked back inside.

"Don't worry," I assured him, placing my hand on the side of his face. "I won't let her get in too much trouble. Outside of the excitement a few months ago, nothing really ever happens in Granville. How much trouble can she get into?"

I leaned up on my tiptoes and kissed him, hoping to take his mind off of Aunt Shirley and her new job. He deepened the kiss and slid his arms around me.

Unfortunately, I was the one that couldn't quiet the voice in the back of my head that said working with Aunt Shirley was going to be a very bad idea.

★★★★★★★★★★

Ready for Book 3 in the Ryli Sinclair Mystery series, Old-Fashioned Murder? Just click here  https://www.amazon.com/gp/product/B071NP1L3R?ref_=dbs_pwh_calw_2&storeType=ebooks !! Happy reading!

ABOUT THE AUTHOR

Jenna writes in the genres of cozy/paranormal cozy/romantic comedy. Her humorous characters and stories revolve around over-the-top family members, creative murders, and there's always a positive element of the military in her stories. Jenna currently lives in Missouri with her fiancé, step-daughter, Nova Scotia duck tolling retriever dog, Brownie, and her tuxedo-cat, Whiskey. She is a former court reporter turned educator turned full-time writer. She has a Master's degree in Special Education, and an Education Specialist degree in Curriculum and Instruction. She also spent twelve years in full-time ministry.

When she's not writing, Jenna likes to attend beer and wine tastings, go antiquing, visit craft festivals, and spend time with her family and friends. You can friend request her on Facebook under Jenna St. James, and don't forget to check out her website at http://jennastjames.com. Be sure to sign up for her newsletter to hear about latest releases.

Made in the USA
Middletown, DE
19 October 2023